For those about to dive into The first book of the 'Laila' trilogy, be warned there are many triggers that can affect you. Talks of self-harm and death are pretty common in this book. Cannibalism and murder are vast themes in this series as well. Not to mention blood sacrifices for satanic rituals. Be very careful once reading this short book. More importantly, look after yourself and enjoy before the Anti-Christ, better known in the book as Masih al Dajjal, arrives to our world.

Please make sure this gets to my brother, Amen.

Hey,

I'm sorry you have to hear from me through a letter but it's too dangerous for me to come to you right now. I don't know how to control it anymore. I'm only me in the day, and then when the sun sets, I can't stop it from controlling me.
Nala can attest to that.
I think the Dajjal's plan is nearing, and I'll be his soon. I can feel him being close to me, but I think he doesn't want to show himself just yet. He likes to play games with me Amen.
So many I forgot what the truth is like.
I never thought It would be like this that I'd turn out this way. I always thought I was strong enough like mama, but I guess all her sacrifices went down the drain huh.
By now I'm sure you know mama was in on it too. Her behaviour towards me makes so much sense now. She didn't want me to be found and I was dumb enough to look through that mirror.

I feel sorry for her but mostly towards you and Nala. You guys don't deserve any of this.

Tell Nala I can't apologise to her because what I did to her brother deserves more than an apology. I know she probably doesn't blame me; she never did.

That night I saw a glimpse of Hell and I know that's where I'll go after the Dajjal is done with me.

I write this knowing it will be my last letter before I lose complete humanity. If you do find this letter, please know that I love you, both of you but that won't stop me from eating you. So, kill me before he makes me kill you. He can make me do just about anything right now.

Uri and Noah will get the Jinn to send you this letter, don't be scared of it, it's one of the good ones.

I made sure no one can open it but you and Nala. The jinn put a spell on it because I'm going to give you instructions to find me and kill me before he consumes me again.

The instructions are down below, it looks blank, but only Nala will be able to see the instructions. Make sure she doesn't say them aloud in case the Queen's jinn's are spying on you.

1.

2.

3.

4.

Amen, remember, I'm not your little sister anymore. I'm not the Laila you once knew. I'll end up in Hell with him if you don't follow my instructions. Soon you'll be begging me to just die.

Hope to see you soon.

Love,

Laila.

Chapter One ~ Midnight Intruder

My eyes feel like their glued together as I wake up

my from a long ritual nap on the living room floor. My homework that was barely complete acted like a makeshift pillow as the TV was still on blaring the usual fantasy, Narnia. It kept me well distracted from all of my assignments that I've left to do last minute, but what's new. It was a Thursday night, the clock reading 10:59pm and the wind is beating down the house once again in a soft display of violence. My dad was sound asleep on the sofa, where he usually stays for the night, unless he begins to frantically yell for us to carry him upstairs.

Christmas was approaching, not that I celebrated but it was my time to soak in the darkness and just sit in silence listening to my thoughts and those dark voices dancing around in my head.

I leave my books on the floor and lower the volume of the tele. It gets too dark and quiet if the TV isn't on, making the house feel like an empty pit of sadness. You could hear every breath someone takes in this house, with its painful stillness. The electric bill was much higher of course but at least the house didn't feel abandoned.

"Night baba"

I wrap a blanket over his almost corpse body. He hasn't died yet of course but his time is approaching, his eyes are sucked into his skull remind me so each day.

I always tell myself how happy he would be if he finally just passed on to the other side. I don't regret having these thoughts even though I know not to say them aloud.

I dreamt of him again last night, he was under a tree with mama and lilies were surrounding their fragile bodies. They looked so young and healthy laying there that I almost didn't recognise them, plagued by their pale sick faces and sorrow eyes.

They kept staring at the clear sky above them that intertwined in angelic colours as I went unnoticed. It was truly peaceful, and I finally didn't shed a tear in who knows how long.

I tucked him in yesterday and he motioned for me to come closer to him, his skeletal fingers barely able to point at me. He said "Take me" in my ear probably imagining I was God, able to lift him away from his miserable life. I knew he didn't need to be here anymore, but I can tell he's troubled to leave me and Amen alone. Like he used to say our lives are in God's hands, He decides when to take you. Sometimes baba still recognises us but often when he looks at me, he'd yell and scream as if I was the Angel of Death. The Angel of death in Islam was described to be very frightening and that's how he'd look at me like he was in fear of me.

With Amen however he would just look at him confused till he finally remembers him; I don't think he'll ever remember me.

This all started after mum died a year ago. She had zero health problems, so it took us by surprise. We didn't know how to take the news some of us laughed, some of us cried. One minute she was taking a nap and the next she wouldn't wake up, her body completely soulless. She was dead, whilst we just carried on in the house thinking it was just a normal day; you can imagine what an unexpected demise can do to someone's sanity.

I constantly thought of how selfish it was for God to take her from us so suddenly but at least she wasn't in pain like baba is in now. So really, I should be grateful right?

But I didn't even get the chance to give her the gift I was saving up for her to prove to her I was actually a good daughter.

She was meant to get her favourite necklace on New Year's, her birthday. I wrapped it around my neck on her funeral and its stayed there since. A necklace in the shape of a moon, I liked it, it suited me. I remember she'd stop by this Indian Jewel shop every Sunday when we'd do our grocery shop. It would grab her attention so quickly that she'd get whiplash every time, so we'd stop, and I'd listen to her sulk about how she could never afford something so expensive.

It quickly became apparent how life was so dull without her and more apparent how horribly we handled her death. After we buried her in Algeria my dad fell ill, he couldn't do it anymore. I mean none of us really could, I had to pinch myself till I bled, to realise this was real.

First, he wanted to stay with her, he spent a month by her grave and we eventually had to force him out when we had to come back to London. He could barely form a sentence at her funeral. He stared at the floor the whole time when people came to pay their respects, Amen had to talk in his expense. I however just stared at her; I could see her sitting beside Baba beautiful as ever. She wasn't really there; however, her figure was almost opaque with a white light surrounding her, but her features were still shining through.

She saw me looking at her, but she didn't smile at me, though she never really smiled at me even when she was alive.

My family probably thought I was just as sad as baba, but I was too preoccupied watching her for hours till sleep took me. I never saw her again when I woke up. She was really gone.

No doctor took dad's health seriously, so eventually he started to lose his voice and ability to move. They didn't know what was wrong with him. He was always so strong, other men were always intimidated by him at work. They said his condition is untreatable and they seemed more confused than we were at the time, so slowly we naturally gave up and welcomed death once again to our door.

Amen was almost numb to it, still coping with mama's death. They were tied to the hip and had the same humour, always leaving me out of their inside jokes unless it was about me of course. He almost became mute if it wasn't for his new job as a police officer. He finally passed the academy, and it was forcing him to escape home and resume to normalcy or pretend at least.

I wish he confided in me more, but I look exactly like mama that he sometimes can't stand to look at me in the daytime.

I kiss baba's scrawny cheeks and make my way upstairs. The carpets in the hallway were barely holding on. I always remind Amen to re do them, but he's been so busy at work he stopped caring about how the house looked like. I could do them myself but I'm skint, every job fires me after a month.

This house is a skinny three-bedroom council estate in Brixton with mouldy walls and a boiler that never fails to break down but at least we didn't live in flat anymore.

I walk inside my room, which feels like a bloody steam room. The heat infecting my lungs as it crawls inside my body.

Amen always has the heating up too high so baba can feel warm, but this winter feel's different. I don't feel that painful cold the U.K offered anymore which seems preposterous because everyone always complains about the weather here. Right now, it's the only thing that feels good. I walk over to my window and open them wide until I can feel my skin escape the warmth. I have a graveyard as my window view across the street, the usual hang out for potheads at night. They've become quiet since my brother joined the police, but I can still hear their whispers every so often. The ice-cold breeze feels sharp on my face as it caresses the room and beats me till I'm red all over. Coated in its frost.

I adjust my hijab on my head just enough so it loose and flows in the wind to wonder across my face. It feels euphoric.

My clothes were scattered everywhere around my bed and there were books in places they shouldn't be.

My room looked like I dumped my trash over it. I hoard all my artwork I created as a child and I'm not ready to get rid of it just yet. I do try to throw it away, but my inner child talks me out of it every time.

All of my walls where painted black, back when I went through my goth phase in the end of high school.

Jaden, my high school crush was a goth and I wanted him to notice me so bad that I became the cringiest hijabi wannabe goth, but he friend zoned me as did every other guy I crushed on after him.

I do wonder if the walls where a brighter colour, would I feel more alive, but all my thoughts now have become anything but bright or alive.

I jump on to my bed in the corner of my room situated right beside my windows and begin to stare out in the night sky, the stars watching over me as I observe them from my tiny room. My hair itching to escape my scarf. I have the unruliest hair, not as curly as my best friend Nala's but just a ball of frizz and waves with no regulations. I hate seeing it.

I lay on top of my bed sheets and soak in the cold December month, closing my eyes and letting the air turn my skin to ice.

I can't help but think of mama when I look at the stars. Sometimes I imagine them as people, and she could be one of them floating around aimlessly. I used to talk to her as if she were a star but then I stopped when I realised no one was talking back to me, so now I just sit here and stare in silence.

I can't even remember how she sounded like; I feel bad not remembering her voice. I had a few videos of her, but I'd rather not open them, feels odd seeing her knowing she's dead.

A light knock on my door snaps me out my thoughts. Only Amen knocks before entering my room unlike Nala who'd just barge in without knocking. We both didn't realise we had trouble sleeping until we'd bump into each other in the kitchen every other night cooking up a meal to distract ourselves from our thoughts.

It was an unspoken confirmation that we had one Friday night when he bought me a plate of fruit to my room, and I was wide awake at 3 am that we both couldn't sleep like we used to. My room became our designated nightly hangout to wait for some sort of sleep to come. Sometimes, we didn't even talk, silence was more than comforting till we passed out or didn't.

"Leela, you up?"

He peeks through the door. His cute little nose sliding through the edge.

"No"

He comes in anyway with his uniform still glued to his body. I know he secretly loves that thing; I barely see him in anything else anymore.

He kicks his shoes off in the corner of my room.

He has a buzzcut that he decided to get last week since Nala said she likes the new guy in sixth form because of his buzzcut. Typical Amen behaviour.

Amen chopped his hair right away. First Nala said she liked surfer guys because of their long hair so Amen was growing, it got super long past his shoulders he had to tie it up most of the time. He didn't even hesitate to cut it off once he heard her talking about the new guy. He's always liked her, but he'd never admit it. She on the other hand didn't even notice or pretended not to.

"Fuck I swear your gonna catch a cold, what's wrong with you?"

Pointing to my windows fully open, he always complains about them.

"At least leave one open, I'm sweating"

He leaves one a little open, even though it's not enough I welcomed the gesture.

"You just wanna be sick and skip school, right?"
Well, he has a point skipping school or better yet dropping out seems like the American dream right now but sadly I'm British and America is far away.

"I'll probably die from a heat stroke in this house"
He ignores me and drops on my bed, his body weight sinking the mattress. Amen can be quite shy around people even with his tall and buff exterior he's more of the sensitive sibling, the total opposite of me. He's the stereotypical Algerian male, never smiles and if he does it has to be deserved but he's very caring and sweet to me, nonetheless.
I'm the total opposite of him, more on the skinny side almost bony and paler in complexion to his slight tanned skin. He has hazel eyes flooded with green and honey and mine are dark as the walls of my room. Not to mention I barely reach his shoulder like Nala does. He's 6ft 3 and Nala was 5'10 on a good day and I was barely 5'5.

"Did you eat?"

"Yeah, I had some water" I smirk.
He rolls his eyes.

"You want me to make you something?"

"No, I was just joking I had some of baba's soup, he didn't finish it again"
Amen sighs and puts his hands under his head whilst looking at me.

"Again?"
I nod and look away. He's nearly stopped eating all together. I didn't want to think about the time coming when

he stops eating all together, but we knew that time would come.

"I actually came home early to make sure you and Nal's aren't going out tonight"

He takes out a cigarette putting it in the tip of his mouth as he searches for his lighter in his pockets looking distressed.

"Why? you could 'a just called to ask"

"I was working in the area anyway"

He doesn't respond to my other question, too preoccupied with finding his lighter that seems to have gone missing. I grab my lighter underneath my pillow and flick it at him.

"Cheers"

He catches it with both hands and lights it up. I wait for him to take a long drag of his cigarette. I stopped smoking cigarettes only smoking weed to get some sleep but sometimes I do miss it, mostly the foul smell.

Amen always smokes when he's in deep thought which he spends most of his day doing but this time his eyebrows are crushed together as he sits on my bed, slumped staring at the trees outside the window with his elbows on his knees and cigarette in between his fingers. He plays with my lighter with his free hand swinging it between his fingers in a translucent dance.

"You remember a month ago when Jane died?"

"Yeah, I remember, everyone here does"

Really how can anyone forget, her killer left her body scattered in pieces all over Brixton, the BBC finally stopped covering it on the news just a few days ago. He drags his cigarette longer this time and turns to stare at me. A stare I don't get too often only when I've gotten too high to comprehend what he's telling me and yet it doesn't

16

exactly sit right with me, he looks just like baba when he does that, and it creeps me out.

"Well, a second victim was found ten minutes away from here, we found just one of her body part's, so I came back to stay with you, they think there's a serial killer in Brixton."

"Wait, what?"

I sit up right on my bed, intrigued by the idea of a serial killer. I mean not that it's nice to have your body cut into pieces but nothing ever this big happens here. Sure, you have the usual gangs you avoid but never a serial killer.

"Do they know who's body part it was?"

He turns to look at me with sad heavy eyes.

"Yeah, it was Lucy's head."

"Lucy…"

"Lucy Cann, she's goes to your school and she's eighteen like you Laila. I don't think you should leave the house for a few days at best."

Lucy wasn't my friend, I didn't have many friends, it was just me and Nala, but Lucy was a girl who would spend most of her days in the Library. Nobody really talked to her, she liked it that way. I know I do.

"How did you find it?"

Amen shakes his head.

"They'll tell you in the news tomorrow. I don't wanna relive today" He yawns.

He looked like someone sucked the soul out of him. Amen and his team also found Jane's body. He was on her case and now having to deal with another one must be tiring.

"So, you came back because you think I won't be safe? come on its usually white people they target, no one's gonna harm me"

17

I didn't sound too convincing my voice shaking slightly at the end giving me away. Amen stands up to flick his cigarette out the window.

"This isn't some joke Laila, if something happens to you…"

He looks away and glares at the street. He's right, if something happened to him, I don't think I could go on living either. Everyone leaving you and then coming back to an empty house with no one to look at or talk to but yourself. I think I'd drive my-self to the mental asylum.

"Sorry" I whisper.

He turns around and leans his back on the window whilst both his hands brush through his hair.

"Anyway, we're sure it's a serial killer, they're gonna announce it in the morning"

I cross my legs on the bed thinking of who it could be.

"Have they found a lead?"

He looks at me and laughs. It doesn't quite reach his eyes, just a painless laugh that's not contagious.

"Yeah, he has middle eastern features"

He raises his eyebrows teasingly.

"Then the killer could be you" I gasp.

We both let out a laugh that's not bombarded with genuine joy just a sound to cut the suffocating tension in the room. We talked about death as if it were the weather, so disastrously numb to it.

"It could be me"

"So, I'm safe?"

He rolls his eyes at me and flicks his cigarette out the window.

"I don't want to take any chances, tell Nala ASAP, I don't want her going out either"

I look at my phone, she hasn't replied to any of my messages that I sent hours ago.

"She said she's sleeping over today but she still hasn't called or left a text"

We both look towards the clock on my door that reads 11:33pm, similar to the time we realised mum died instead it was 6:33pm. What is it with these three's showing up whenever something feels bad?

Amen coughs uncomfortably clearly realising what I'm thinking.

"Maybe give her a call...now" he says looking at my phone.

"She finished work an hour ago she should be here by now raiding the fridge" he adds.

I nod my head picking up my phone to call her when a rock hits the window startling us. Another one following suit.

We run over to see who's throwing them. It's Nala she's waving at us frantically her eyes wide with fear.

"Nala?"

She looked frazzled her hair all up in the sky as she points to the door.

"Shit"

Amen runs downstairs and I follow closely behind as we try our best not to wake up baba whose sound asleep in the living room. Amen opens the door with so much speed to see a horrified and bloodied Nala trying to catch her breath. She looks behind her, terrified. Her face covered in sweat and blood that's dripping down from her head all the way her chin.

"WHAT HAPPENED TO YOU"

Amen clamps his hands over my mouth. I couldn't control my voice; I've never seen Nala this hurt before.

"Sorry, I didn't wanna wake up your dad" Nala whispers.

"What happened"

Amen ushers her inside and closes the door.

Her breathing rapidly increasing as she fights for air. Her blood falling on the carpet. Her top drenched in sweat and her long lean legs look like they're going to pass out any minute now. Amen extends his hand to help her up the stairs but she swats it away like you do to a fly, and she persists to climbs up on her own nearly falling over multiple times.

I open the front door to look outside. She did look behind her. Maybe someone was chasing her, but the streets were empty nobody usually goes out in this neighbourhood at this time.

I close the door gently making sure baba is still sound asleep which he is, coddled in two huge blankets snoring lightly. I walk upstairs to the bathroom to see Nala sitting inside the bathtub with her legs stretched out and her head laid back as she lets Amen clean the blood of her forehead. I shut the door behind me.

"So, Start talking who did this to you"

Amen is gripping the bathtub with his free hand so tightly it might break.

I go over to her and put her curly hair up in a bun. Her Somali genes offering her the silkiest and most voluminous hair that shapes her petite face so elegantly. Amen tenderly wipes her face beside me as he stares at her in deep thought. I know he's worried but he's trying to keep calm because Nala looks like she's about to have a panic attack right now.

"This man was following me after work, and I didn't think much of it because well… he was kinda cute"
She says the last part more to herself, but we still caught it. Amen rolls his eyes.

"I'll get you an ambulance" Amen says quietly as he throws the wipes at me and goes on his phone.
I offer her some water and she swing's it back. Gulping it down to the last droplets as if she were fasting all day. Me and Amen watch her intently out of concern to what she might say next. A serial killer is already on the loose and me Nala are in the age range of the victims so I can only assume Amens serious detective look is to do with that. Nala opens her eyes to look at me. Her stare so piercing and alluring although I'm straight as a stick, Nala could get it…twice.

"You know how I start reading the Quran at night when I'm walking home just so the jinn's don't follow me"

"Yeah, and?" I ask.
Nala laughs and focuses on Amen who's standing by the sink.

"Don't laugh at me Amen but I think a jinn just fuckin' attacked me" she says to him.

"A jinn? Nala don't play with me today"

"NO, I'm serious Amen I'm not playing, stop thinking I'm crazy"
He sighs reaching for another cigarette, but I snatch it away from him.

"Seriously hurry up" I say, frustrated at the long pauses and weird eye contact going on between them.

"Alright so I get the munchies after work because I got high as fuck during my break, so I go to Tesco to get some snacks when this hot guy pushes in front of me and pays for me"

"How hot" I interrupt.

"Like Ben Affleck if he was Arab"

I look at Amen and he looks back at me his Jaw clenched.

"Anyway, then he keeps following me out the store, but he doesn't even say anything to me. He just follows me all the way near the round-about"

"He was following you for a while and you didn't think to call us?"

Amen was on the verge of hitting something.

"Sorry I spaced. So anyway, I'm kinda freaked out so I take a detour to where all of Jadon's friends all smoke. I thought I'd better be with them if anything happened to me"

She hands me the empty glass and continues.

"Wait you sure he looked Arab?" Amen asks.

"Yes, but kinda pale, too pale kinda like Laila" Nala laughs.

I roll my eyes.

"I'm not that pale" I say as I touch my pale face.

Amen starts typing on his phone, probably alerting his colleagues of the serial killer he told me about.

"Yeah, sure Leel's, anyways as I was saying I walked to where Jaden and his friends hang out and they weren't there and to top it all off the guy is still following me"

She closes her eyes and takes a deep breath. I hold on to her hands, her fingers intertwining with mine as she opens her eyes again to the ceiling avoiding any eye contact with us.

"But their always there?"

"Right, but what's even strange is that no one was there. The streets where so empty. When have you ever seen those estates empty at night?"

I shrug. She was right everyone was usually out at this time, smoking or drinking at the estates.

"It was just me and him, but I wasn't that scared yet because you know how fast I could run, I thought if I started legging it now, I'd make it to yours in five."

"Show off"

"Yeah, I feel Kenyan sometimes"

Amens legs were moving up and down impatiently.

"Anyways, I legged it, but he made it in front of me in no time, he was so fast it didn't even seem like he was trying. I could have sworn I saw his eyes turn black, so I started to recite the Quran thinking this gotta be a demon and THEN his face... I can't describe it, but it looked like it was burning, like smoke started coming out of his skin"

"Smoke?" Amen asks.

"Yeah, it freaked me out"

Me and Amen exchanged glances not sure what to make of what she's saying or even to believe her. You can usually tell when Nala lies, her eyebrows start to twitch, and they weren't twitching right now.

"How high did you get?" Amen asks.

Nala gives him a deadpan look.

"So, his face was on... fire?" I interrupt.

"I told you guys, please don't think I'm crazy"

"We don't think you're crazy but that doesn't explain the blood Nala" I try to comfort her.

"Well after he started...burning he was grabbing his face in pain, so I ran so fast, probably the fastest I've ever ran, and I couldn't hear him running after me, so I thought I was safe… but… he caught up to me again and I didn't even hear him, he was so silent. He was grabbing me by my neck, but this is the weird part right"

"What his skin burning wasn't weird?" I joke.
She stops to looks at us not finding my joke funny at all. I'm sure we look like two confused siblings looking at her as if she were telling us aliens had kidnapped her and did experiments on her and the government was hiding it.

"No that wasn't as weird as what he did next"
She sits up in the bathtub, wincing as she does so and takes a deep breath.
Amen crouches back down.

"What did he do?" he says gently.

"He bit my neck" she breaths.
He grabs her face and twists it to see her neck.

"Don't"
She pushes his hands off her face and proceeds to shed some tears.

"He keeps digging his teeth into my neck and all I can do is start doing the shahada because I thought well, I was gonna die and I don't wanna go to hell. Man, my life just felt like it was gonna end right there. It felt like someone was drilling holes in me. I couldn't even scream the way I wanted to, it was like he paralyzed me, and all I was thinking of was that I haven't even prayed in so long that I'm definitely going straight to hell"
Nala always makes a joke out of any serious situation and normally I'd laugh back but I just can't bring myself to when she said he bit her neck.

"What like some vampire shit?"

"Laila it's not funny"

"Then what?" Amen asks.

24

"This random Jewish Geezer saved me"

"Jewish?"

"He was bold apart from those two hairs that they let out in the front, and he was wearing a Kippa, I think that's what it's called. He just tore the guy away from me and told me to run, so I did and now I'm in your bathtub smelling like blood and piss"

I look at her Neck there was no wounds or scars, it was smooth. Only her head was bleeding possibly from the man hitting her. But she had no bite marks. I'm sure the police won't believe her story of the biting, but she sure enough was man handled. Her long sleeve, waiter shirt missing a few buttons and her trousers ripped in the knee.

"Nala, there's no bite marks
on your neck"

She feels her smooth neck.

"How? he was literally tearing at my neck a few minutes ago"

"Maybe you hit your head when he caught up to you?" Amen asks.

Amen's phone rings and he walks out to answer it.

"Or maybe you took more than just weed?" I tease.

Nala hits me on the head.

"If so then what about the Jew that helped me huh?"

She gets up to look at the mirror and rinses her neck with water. She looked confused and serious, a close reflection of Amen when he's in deep thought. She holds on to her neck and looks at me through the mirror.

"When do you ever see a Jew in Brixton, aren't they up north?"

"Laila he was biting me, it felt like he was drilling into my neck, I mean I could have sworn he hit a bone or something"

I hug her from the back, placing my head in between her neck that didn't apparently get bit. She can never lie about something this big, but I've definitely hallucinated taking some drugs her brother used.

"Amen did say there's a serial killer in the area"

"No way!"

"Yeah, and he looks Arab"

Amen comes back in.

"The ambulance are five minutes away, their gonna check your head in case you lost it you lesbo's"

He cringes at us hugging.

Nala attempts to kick him, but he dodges.

"Is it true then, a serial killer in Brixton?"

Amen looks at me disappointed and takes a deep breath.

"Yeah, um we found Lucy Cann's…head today, it's the same as Jane's death"

Nala looks at him paralyzed, her eyes and mouth hanging down, gravity unable to hold them up.

"Her neck, what was it like?"

Amen looks down avoiding her eyes.

"There were several marks on them but that doesn't mean-"

"Yes, it does Amen"

"You don't have any on yours" he sighs.

"But I swear he-"

"Come, I'll make you some food, I told the police everything they're looking around the area, just don't think about it for now"

Amen puts his arm around her shoulders and moves her away from me and to the stairs leaving me in the bathroom alone, staring at my reflection in the mirror.

I move my scarf to see my bare neck and I trace my fingers along my veins to my collar bones.

I place my nails into the crevasses. My sharp nails digging into it, trying to feel how painful it would be if someone bit inside of it.

Truth be told hearing Nala talk about him and the pain she felt reminded me of a time I felt the most alive. The adrenaline from her story however was not enough for me, I want more, I want to actually feel what she went through.

I catch my eyes in the mirror which make me halt the assault of my neck.

They were turning black.

Mama did tell me that mirrors where portals between us and the spiritual world and she would warn me not to look at myself for too long. When she did catch me staring at myself, she would beat me.

She would get out her belt, it was the only time she actually hit me, but she ended up stopping once she realised, I liked the pain. I accidently smiled through it, and she saw. She later smashed all the mirrors in the house.

Once she died, we finally bought a mirror for the bathroom. She always looked scared when I was in the bathroom alone. She didn't even let me have mirrors even when I got older, but she allowed Amen to have one. It was small.

She once said it could let Jinn's come out and possess me. I don't how true that was, but my eyes right now where beyond their normal deep brown, they were transforming to black even the veins inside where slowly turning dark.

I touch my eyes going close up to the mirror. I looked like a demon. I slightly smile at my reflection in the mirror my eyes staring back at me. I look so drastically different nothing compared to how I looked with my normal eyes. I'm almost possessed by them, their contrast to my skin was alluring.

The mirror begins to cloud in a black smoke as my reflection blends into it.

"Fuck"

I touch the mirror which has now become completely pitch black, but my reflection was still there even though it was dim. My eyes looked hollow beside the mirror. It was scary but hypnotising.

I can feel the ground on my bare feet beginning to feel different. It was no longer my cold bathroom tiles, instead it felt like I was on soil. I can feel mud in between my toes but I can't see any.

I hear a faint scream right beside my right ear and I look up at the mirror where a young boy is thrashing around. His arms were tide to his body in chains and his mouth couldn't move because It was sewed together. His eyes were stained with tears as he makes eye contact with me through the mirror.

"Guys Come up here"

I don't know if I'm hallucinating but if Amen and Nala can see what I'm seeing then I'll feel less insane right now.

The lights in the bathroom switch off on their own and the bathroom door slams shut. Now it's just me and the boy alone in the darkness.

He looks at me through the mirror with hope, his eyes begging me to save him as he thrashes in the ground. His face so dirty and scared but my eyes are simply captivated by the people around him. I can hear the trees thrashing sounds as if I were actually there. Heavy chanting also filled my eardrums but made my chest feel tight with pain, but I wanted to see more.

Chapter Two ~ The sacrifice

In the heart of a solitary forest near the Middle East, all creatures from the physical and spiritual world where as still as Laila is, staring into her mirror. Their eyes and ears on full alert for the danger they know will come.

A young boy that couldn't be any older than ten years old was in the most exhausting pain that he has ever been in. He's chained from his feet to his hands in ropes that are drenched in poison, eating away at his skin making him irritable and out of control.

His red cheeks were drenched in his tears and his body was only dressed in a piece of white cloth that only did enough to hide his lower body.

He can see Laila's reflection in the sky above him as he prays in his head for God to bring someone to save him. Her reflection quickly disappears as she moves on to watching those around him, diminishing that little speck of hope he had left in his mind.

Maybe the only way God could save him is if he died right now, he thought. He was kidnapped in his sleep and woke up to women with teeth as long as his arms tying him to the ground.

Around him were masked men sitting crossed legged circling the terrified boy and chanting in Aramaic.

They're praying for their Lord, Iblis the one who created them.

These masked people are far from human, their entire bodies draped in a curtain of black robes, hiding every inch of their skin as their heads dance in rhythmic synchronized movements up and down, swaying from left to right.

Their chants becoming louder by the second. Saliva was dripping out of their mouth, hungry to feast on the boy but he was not meant to be feasted on tonight.

A five shaped star digs through the grounds soil and forms it's shape around the boys fragile body.

His mouth was stitched tightly shut so he could only whine and let his tears run to the grass under neath him hoping to be relieved from this evil.

All of a sudden, the air shifts in the forest warning every being of new arrivals as the wind sways viciously around the trees.

Hundreds of witches begin to emerge in a puff of black smoke behind the cloaked chanters as they position themselves behind bushes peeping at the boy in the centre. They all wore niqabs to stay hidden from any humans who wanted to interrupt their Journeys to Iblis.

If they were caught by any Muslims, they'd be burnt alive. Some witches travelled all over Africa and the Middle East just to get here and witness their Lord in the flesh.

Some of these women sold themselves to Iblis at a young age. He saved them from poverty and now they hold high ranks in the Kingdom. Their job was to protect and worship Him all night.

They all had a jinn attached to their backs making sure no one was capable of worshipping Allah, the creator of the universe. Betraying Iblis would mean the end of you and your loved ones, dying slowly and painfully.

The Jinn's glued to them from behind were only visible to sorcerers and non-humans thus allowing the witches to go undetected in the physical world.

There's more than a hundred of them now behind the cloaked ones all of them ready for what's to come.

They get rid of their gloves and their niqabs and hold on to each other's hands, forming a bigger circle around the open forest.

It was pitch black only the moonlight was bright enough to light a pathway to see what was happening.

The enormous trees hindering any prying eyes from intruding on such a sacred ceremony, but Laila went unnoticed even by the Witches who see everything and everyone.

They fill the corners of the forest leaving no room for anyone to enter by holding on to each other's hands and whispering a prayer with their eyes closed. Their eyelids moving uncontrollably as they begin chanting to the demons around the forest. Summoning all the power from the darkness.

An invisible gate traps everyone inside the circle, not allowing any creature in the woods to enter even if they wanted to.

The chants of the cloaked ones became louder, and their heads were swaying widely in perfect harmony with the witches prayers.

From the heightened elevation of vibrational chants, a ball of black fire came out of the boys mouth. His stitches tear open to let out the black fire that reached the top of the tree's, skimming the sky.

His eyes were shaking, horrified as he looked up at the fire escaping his mouth.

A treacherous howl makes it way to the woods.

It was a herd of centaurs charging towards the fire trying to barge through the witches binding circle but to no luck, the gate was too powerful to break into, even for their strength and powerful numbers.

Hundreds of centaurs restlessly look at the boy's flame. They're howls becoming deafening as they await behind the witches unable to break through to the boy and eat him alive. The centaurs where controlled by their appetite, especially since the Vampire Queen doesn't allow them to eat freely.

Only a boy before puberty was to be sacrificed for Iblis to come out. Iblis's body was only in the spiritual world, making it hard for him to be summoned to the physical realm without a blood sacrifice. He enjoyed little boys especially more than girls.

The cloaked ones take of their masks and hang their teeth wide open. They can only become Vampires in their pure form once their father is close to them.

They can feel Iblis coming through to the physical world as Jinn's flock to the vampires and await him. Their mouths drooling at the sight of the boy. The fire spreads around the boy following the star around him and to his forehead.

The ground begins to rumble, and the trees begin to sway angrily as the forest hates Iblis's presence inside of it. The centaurs too become restless thrashing behind the witches, utterly possessed by the boys black fire that's crawling up his body and shutting down all of his organs.

He becomes consumed by the Jinn's fire, his body almost lost in it completely.

Suddenly the chanting comes to a stop, the witches begin to age rapidly their true form coming to light. They were old and wrinkly.

The cloaked ones slowly take off their black veils revealing their pale faces and red eyes. Theirs about a hundred of them circling the boy.

All of them have red eyes yet one man, Noah who has eyes as black as there veils and hair as dark as the night with a scar across his left eye that plunges down his cheek and stops at his chin. He watches the boy's body deteriorate into the black fire with no remorse or sympathy. His face so dangerously still, listening to the boys screams as blood gushed out of his eyes and he melts into the ground. The witches shriek with pleasure at the sight that was like ecstasy to them, pleased by their magic.

The only remains of the boy were his blood. In the boys absence Iblis finally stretches out from the ground and stands up, licking the boys blood from his fingers. He looks like the Centaurs taking the shape of their horse like feet, but the rest of his body stands tall and muscular with two large horns on his head. His eyes were black like the fire. The black smoke that wraps around him allowing only half of his face to be seen and covers his private parts. Iblis's nose breaths out smoke as he stands like a beast inside the star looking down at his worshippers.

His right eye was still shut but the veins on his eyelids thrash around, ready to be awakened. His presence brings calm to the Centaurus and other creatures hiding in the forest. They stand in silence in front of him. It was a great pleasure for them to actually see him in the flesh.

Whenever a ceremony like this happens which was rare, it would bring them to tears but today was different.

Everyone was dying with excitement. They were close to the end times, and they needed to do one last thing before the prophecy was truly completely.

"The father has been summoned"
Ezekiel, a man amongst the vampires.
A high-ranking cloaked man to first instruct everyone to bow to Iblis with their heads touching the ground.

"ALL HAIL IBLIS" Ezekiel shouts.
His eyes twinkling in the moonlight as he stares at the beautiful creature, they call Father. Everyone cheers. The men and women in cloaks all go down and put their heads on the floor, but the witches don't. They back away behind the trees and lower their heads and watch from afar.
The trees stop swaying with emotional distress and wrap there leaves closely to them in distain.
Iblis finally opens his right eye, a dark red like his horns with a bright red a flame in his pupils. He begins to raise his left hand and points it at Noah who's kneeling in front of him between other men.

"Rise"
His voice echoed around the forest. It sucked away any hope you had left and shattered your soul empty leaving it to only attach yourself to him. Laila backed away to the witches, she was barefoot and scared at seeing him. His body took up most of the forest, and his voice hurt her soul. She wants to leave but she doesn't know how.
Noah does as he's told, standing up from his head on the ground. He looks at Iblis's legs and waits as everyone also slowly rises after him.
Iblis points to another vampire this time a woman with beautiful long brown hair and face so pale it would make humans uncomfortable to look at.

"Aaliyah" Iblis points to her.

She bravely looks him in the eye, her hunger for power dripping out of her. His eyes burning into her skull, but she keeps hold of the eye contact and doesn't waver no matter the pain.

"You are to mate with Noah, the future King"

He points to Noah who looks at Aaliyah to his right with discontent.

Noah never particularly liked her but if it meant he will be King then no questions asked he would do it. He knew he had a soulmate that could lose her soul if he mated with another, but it would be worth it to be the King of Jerusalem.

He's come so far, so another sacrifice would not stop him from achieving his life goal even at the expense of the soul of his other half.

As long as he doesn't meet her before the mating ceremony, he knew he wouldn't think twice about it. Though something about mating with Aaliyah felt unsettling, her voice was so quiet like a mouse, and she was always serious only focusing on winning ever since she was young.

However, he knew Aaliyah would be the perfect Queen for him and the Kingdom. She was skilled in many ways just like Noah. The Vampire kingdom highly feared her just like they did him. No one ever dared try to be on Aaliyah's bad side. Even though she was parentless she was raised as the right hand to the Queen, so her rank was higher than Noah's.

"Come forward you two and Bare your fangs for your Lord." Ezekiel instructs the two.

Noah and Aaliyah walk inside the star flame in front of Iblis as it burns into their skin, they make sure not to show any reaction to it.

All eyes were on them in case they showed an ounce of fear. No one was allowed to be this close to Iblis if they were weak and not capable to handle his sickening flame. Iblis looks at them intently, his eyes are the only thing that he allows to be exposed on his face as the smoke from his nose continues to feed him with life.

The witches begin to holler as Noah and Aliyah stand facing each other and bare the fangs at one another. An intimate initiation that they are willing to sacrifice two souls to Iblis for greater power and allegiance to their Lord. Noah's fangs are wide and sharp whilst Aliyah's are long and thin, the complete opposites and normal for those that aren't soulmates.

A soulmate should have similar features like their fangs and eyes showing that they belong together in earth and in Heaven.

Any being that sacrifices for Satan shall do the opposite of what's naturally ordained.

   "For both of your sacrifices of your other halves, you will be given eternal power. Once you fulfil your promise your debt will be gone from me, and I will make sure your life is eternal"

Iblis raises his left hand with only his first two fingers standing up.

Thousands of Jinn's run to him and present him a gold crown drenched in blood of the sacrificed boy. The jinn's where all in different shapes taking the form of anything that appealed to their eyes.

Iblis hands the crown to Aliyah with one of his large fingers, she takes it gracefully, bowing before him.

"Thank you, Father"

This crown represents the millions of humans that they have killed for the future Kingdom and thus will have great prosperity ruling over the humans in the Middle East. It's energy was the darkest anyone has ever seen radiating through its jewels.

She places it on Noah's head carefully, it was fragile and small on Noah.

He watches detached by the gesture.

Iblis hands over a ring to Noah which he takes from his long claws and turns to look at Aliyah with her fangs still hanging eager to become the Queen.

He hesitates for a second and looks around him, the witches and centaurs are bent over staring with mouths agape at him and Aaliyah. Everyone in the kingdom was silently watching them and he knew his life would change from this moment onwards. He will finally have a lasting rank in the Kingdom and not just the son of someone who once had a rank.

Excitement filled in all the vampires faces as they wait with wide beady eyes for him to put the ring on Aaliyah. There were more vampires in black cloak's near the centaurs now. They couldn't watch from inside, but no one wanted to miss seeing Iblis, there Lord that was shunned from Heaven.

As he goes to turn back to Aaliyah her features begin to disappear.

Laila doesn't know what possessed her, but her legs move on their own as she stands Infront of Noah going through Aaliyah's body.

Now with black oval eyes and her hair hidden in a black scarf staring at him in disbelief. Her features become more prominent, and freckles begin to cover her nose and her lips become so blood red and full. Her eyes so alluring and mystical the complete opposite of Aaliyah's.

Laila is the girl he's seeing, staring back at him with her eyebrows knitted together, confused on how she entered Aaliyah's body.

She takes over the body and extends her hand out for the ring her body moving without her consent. Noah looks back around, no one notices what was happening. He tries his best to mask his emotions as he puts the ring on Laila her hands feeling so soft on his. He thought he was hallucinating but she felt so real next to him, and her touch was like electricity dancing in his veins. Her warmth making him jittery and uncontrollable. His senses on the verge to rip her body open and lick every inch of her organs.

The witches cheer and the vampires hail in the joy at the exchange of the ring. He feels her hand in his as the ring fits her perfectly. Her warmth was like a human, but her eyes were like his, she had to be like him he thought.

Laila likes his touch and moves into him but as she does so, she feels herself quickly disappearing, and Aliyah is now standing in front of him waiting to be eaten by him. He takes a step back wondering where the girl went.

"What?" Aaliyah mouths.

Noah bends his head to Aaliyah for her to put the crown on him, but she already had. She pushes him back up, and he realises his mistake shaking his head. Aaliyah was back and the girl that was just in her place is gone. His mind was frazzled.

Noah stands there puzzled with his eyes glazed over asking himself if he hallucinated just now or was, that girl real. Her beauty was like one of a human, but her eyes were like his, a demon. Could it have been…he shakes his head his thoughts leading him to a dangerous path.

"Now drink from each other" Iblis instructs.

Aliyah comes closer to Noah and extends her neck to which he does the same and they bite down on one each other's neck's causing a rippled effect of pleasure as they begin to suck the blood out of each other's veins, drinking it with the utmost greed.

The Veins on their faces start to expand out of their skin from the ecstasy of drinking blood. Everyone watches intently at the sacred art of vampires feasting from each other that can only be done in front of Iblis and no one else. This feast represents their devotion to their Lord and their entire abandonment of the creator.

Laila's face plagues Noah's mind as he feasts on Aaliyah. What would her blood taste like? He thought.

Aaliyah's blood tasted sour and dry, he liked it to be sweet for him to drink with content.

The witches begin to vanish in an air of dust and Satan slowly hunches on all fours and dissolves in his black flame into the ground.

The first initiation ceremony for Noah to be the future king is complete and most importantly successful.

The Centaurs run back inside the forest whilst the other vampires cover their heads with their hoods and vanish away from the scene with their lightning speed. Leaving Aliyah and Noah alone, their mouths and chins covered in each other's blood as they eye each other up and down.

"I'll see you at the mating ceremony" she says unaffected by his lack of words.

He nods at her and watches her put her hood on and disappear into the forest, her speed completely unmatched by anyone else.

Noah stands alone in the centre of the woods wiping her blood of his face with resentment. The silence feels unnatural, but he's used to it. He looks around to see if the girl was still here, but it was just him left alone.

The grass begins to grow quickly hiding the star that dug into the ground and the trees in the forest begin to stretch their leaves, sighing loudly that Iblis is gone.

He takes of the crown on his head and looks at it with a sly smile on his face.

"Finally,"

He wipes the crown clean from the boys blood.

A man walks into the forest holding another man by the neck interrupting Noah's moment alone.

"Uri?"

Noah squints his eyes to get a better look at him.

Uri, a semi bold man with two long curly hairs hanging down from his temples and a kippa on his head smiles at Noah. He had a long ginger beard, and his hands were covered in fresh scars.

"Hi brother"

Noah smiles at him and hugs him, completely ignoring the man who's badly injured in Uri's right hand.

"You missed it"

Uri rolls his eyes.

"I wasn't invited"

A smile on Noah's face is foreign to anyone but Uri.

They're not exactly blood brothers but they were raised by

the same parents. Uri was an orphan who worked for Noah's family when he was ten and soon adopted by Noah's parents who turned him into a vampire when he turned eighteen.

"Who's this?"

Noah points to the man that Uri holds on to from the back of his neck, Uris claws digging deep into his skin.

"The one that's been killing those girls in London"

"Mmm your famous now lad" Noah says to the man.

Noah bends down and looks at his deformed face.

"You missed the ceremony to get this guy?"

"He's been spreading a rumour about you"

Noah raises his right eyebrow.

"Your father also told me to find him"

Uri never called Noah's father his own, he was never really allowed to.

"He did? why didn't he tell me"

"I'm not sure but he told me not to tell you, but I don't see the harm in you knowing"

Uri shrugs.

"That's weird"

Noah stares at the man grabbing onto his mouth and grips on to one of his fangs. He rips it out in one soft motion making the man's screams fill the thick silence of the forest as Noah holds his tooth and digs into his neck. He weeps in pain at his lost fang.

"P…Please" the man begs.

Noah laughs at him.

"How dare you spread rumours about me, your future King"

Noah reaches for his other fang, if he rips out both of them, he would be a toothless vampire. He would be an easy prey to anyone coming near him.

"I...I found her" he stutters.

"Found who?"

Uri puts more pressure on the man's neck.

"He's just waffling Noah"

Noah ignores Uri and proceeds to hold on to the man's last fang, gripping it with so much force it could crack at any moment.

"Who did you find?"

Noah looks between Uri and the man, his jaw clenched tightly.

"Your rightful Queen" his voice cracks.

Blood is pouring down from his mouth, but he smiles through the pain. A beaten face and one less fang yet he looks' at Noah from his puffy purple eyes with so much joy.

"Your other half" he hisses.

Noah lets go of his fang making the man loose balance.

"My mate?"

Noah looks to Uri in disbelief.

Uri shakes his head.

"Trust me, he's just lying he's been saying that the whole journey here"

The man shakes his head. His hands tied behind him begging Uri with his eyes.

"How would you even know his mate" Uri spits.

"Right how would you know her?"

"All I know...is that she follows Mohammed"

Noah and Uri knew what he meant. She was a Muslim and indeed Noah remembers the girl he just saw. She wore a hijab and carried herself like a believer but how would this man know.

"How do you know her?"

"Oh, come on bro, you're not actually believing this shit"

"Uri stop"

Noah grabbed the man by the neck.

"Answer me"

He looks at Noah, his face so close to his that their noses touch.

"There's a lot of us that want our future King to be with the right Queen"

There was a huge shift in opinion between vampires, some wanting Noah to be with his rightful Queen instead of Aaliyah chosen by Iblis, but no one dared to go against the Queen and Iblis.

"Our father has spoken; your Queen will be Aaliyah"

"He's not my father"

Noah tightens his grip around his neck.

"How dare you say that. He has given us eternal power and life"

"Not all of us want that kind of power. We want peace in the future Kingdom"

"And you will get peace once I'm king"

The man shakes his head.

"No, you won't, anything that comes from Iblis always has a price"

"Okay sorry to interrupt but how on earth could you have found his mate again?"

Uri interrupts, his arms crossed together.

"Yeah, how did you find her?"

The man gulps.

"I can't, l could be killed if I speak"

"I can rip out your last fang and you'll be good as dead if you don't speak"

He looks to Uri pleading him with his eyes.

"You heard him"

The man sighs as he looks back at Noah, his face deadly. His fangs were extended to the bottom of his chin and his eyes becoming darker by the second.

"A lot of people are looking for your mate Noah"

"Why are they looking for her? Just because they want her to be Queen?"

Noah and Uri look at him confused, they know Iblis holds power to the Kingdom and so does the Queen.

"To keep her safe of course"

"Safe from who?"

Uri sighs.

"From the Beast"

"Alright he's clearly messing with us now"

Uri grabs the back of his neck again, frustrated by the man's answers.

"I don't think he's messing with us"

The man smiles at them.

"So, what that justifies him killing those girls"

"No, I didn't kill them I was set up"

Uri rolls his eyes.

"I saw you rip her head out, you didn't even hide it properly"

"Somebody came to my room and poisoned me. Their face was covered but it was definitely another vampire, I could smell her"

"Her?"

"Yes, it happened so fast, one minute I was sleeping the next I was hunting. Somebody clearly didn't want me to find your mate, they wanted to get to her first before I did"

"So, who is she then, my mate"

"I was only able to find her friend. Her mother put a spell on her so she's a hard one to find. Every time I got close; she would disappear"

"Don't forget to mention how you nearly killed her friend too if I didn't stop you in time"

"Her friend was definitely not human; I couldn't bite into her the same as you would a human"

Someone else was in the forest and they could smell them. It was unfamiliar but they were all on edge.

Noah puts his finger on his lips and closes his eyes and listens carefully. The forest was quiet, but a pair of feet were walking on the ground ever so lightly.

Noah opens his eyes and looks at Uri, concern all over his eyes.

"Someone's here"

Uri looks behind him, someone in the end of the forest was moving away from them, making the trees move along with them. Uri's eyesight was better than Noah's because of his left eye that was slightly scarred, but Noah's hearing was stronger.

Uri turns back to Noah and grabs the man by his collar.

"Yalla"

Chapter Three ~ The Loop

What I just witnessed was truly the most disturbing nightmare I have ever stumbled into. My bathroom mirror returns back to normal, the black cloud fading away.
I hug myself and look back at my reflection, my eyes were back to normal so naturally human. But what I saw in there, the people, the beast, were utterly inhuman. A different dimension of creatures with teeth so big and yet faces just like mine.
I rub my eyes because I don't want to go back there. I looked just him. Iblis called him Noah. I could feel him touch me, he knew I didn't belong there and soon he couldn't see me anymore. He looked relieved as if he hadn't gone mad.
Even Iblis couldn't see me crawl up to him. His presence provoked me, like I've known him for a long time ago.
I hear Amen and Nala running up the stairs, Nala gets to me first as she shakes my body that's glued in place, my eyes glaring at my reflection. My eye bags were heavy and unsettled.
   "Why did you shout so loud? Baba's sleeping"
How can I tell them what just happened without sounding like I didn't belong in a mental asylum or better yet jail?
If I described what I just witnessed, I know they wouldn't laugh or shake it off as me being silly. Amen would start

over thinking instead and tell me to get therapy but I know what I saw and felt just now.

Not to mention Nala's story was already ridiculous but at least she had evidence. She came to us with her head bleeding, who wouldn't believe her?

At least the part without the man biting her neck which I believe her now because that man, Noah was biting mine.

I turn to look at their faces and confirm that I shouldn't tell them, with Nala's eyebrows reaching her hairline and Amen looking more pissed than ever.

"Sorry I... I thought I saw something"

I try to feign a smile.

My smile doesn't quite reach my eyes but with everything that happened with Nala they let it go.

"Wait what took you guys so long to come up?"

They look completely baffled.

"What do you mean you called like a few seconds ago"

That can't be right. I felt like I was in that place for at least an hour. I had to watch the boy be in pain for so long that his image is practically framed in my head.

An ambulance disrupts our conversation as it stops right outside our door and it's too loud to bear.

"Arrghhh"

"What's wrong."

"FUCK"

It feels like someone drilling inside my ear lobes.

"You guys can't hear that?"

The ambulance stops its noise and I let go of my ears, sighing loudly.

"I mean its loud but nothing you're not used to" Amen says.

"What's that supposed to mean"

He looks at me with a hint of guilt.

"I'll open the door" he says quietly.

He goes downstairs leaving me and Nala alone. She slants her head to the left, crossing her hands as she does so.

48

"So?" she asks.

I shrug my shoulders.

"So, how's your head?"

"Don't try to change the subject, I haven't seen you this bothered since"

She doesn't finish her sentence, but she looks around the room uncomfortably trying to avoid where the conversation was leading to.

"Since mama died...yeah well like I said I just thought I saw something"

"Are you sure? Because your eyes look like they're about to fall out any second now"

"Just leave it"

"You screamed though babe"

"Okay seriously Nala just-"

"Just tell me what you at least thought you saw then"

I shake my head profusely.

"No"

She'd think I'm crazy.

"What's the time?"

She looks at me with one eyebrow raised.

"Time for you to get a watch"

"No seriously Nala what's the time"

"It's 11:59" she says with a frown.

"Can't be" I say more to myself.

I mean how has time not moved at all here. Everything was so agonisingly slow even my legs feel tired from standing and watching them melt that boy away.

I hug my body confused with what just happened.

"Nala, I don't think I'm ok"

She reaches over to me and puts her hands over my arms.

"Yeah, I'm not either"

"What did you say the man did to your neck?"

I looked her straight in the eye. She looks taken back; her eyes shiny like she's about to cry again.

"He um bit into it, why?" she says too quickly.

"I think I... you know what let's just get you to the ambulance, Amens probably waiting for us"
She rolls her eyes.

"Laila, I swear if you don't spill, I, will fuckin bite YOUR neck off"
I take a deep breath and step away from her and I look directly at the mirror and stare at my reflection again.

"Imma sound crazier than you, but… I just saw a boy melt and then they were doing some sort of ritual to summon Iblis. Then these people that looked like humans but…but had these long teeth were biting each other's necks and then there were these witches"
I pause to glance at Nala's reflection making sure she's following everything I'm saying but instead, she looks completely afraid.

"There were demons too, I could see them, I saw all of it and I think one of them saw me"
Nala gets a text, interrupting me.

"Amen's telling us to come down" she breaths heavily.
I rub my eyes and turn to Nala defeated.

"It sounds crazy right?"

"Laila whatever you saw"

"I know, I know, it's stupid, I probably just imagined it"
She pulls down her jumper to show her smooth neck.

"I know what I saw and what he did to me, but I can't even fuckin prove it, I sound even more crazy than you do"

"Were his teeth"

"Yes" Nala interrupts.
She comes towards me.

"It was like a demon Laila"
A tear leaves her right eye as she hugs me.

"Let's just go down and forget it happened"
I nod and wipe her teary eyes as I grab her hands into mine and lead her downstairs.

A handsome paramedic and Amen are talking at the entrance of the door. The man wore a hat, but you can tell he didn't have much hair, but he does have a full connecting beard and these green eyes that sort of feel familiar.

I wonder if I've seen him before. He was taller than Amen and more on the skinny side. They both notice us.

"This is Nala, the one that hit her head"

He watches me instead and Amen notices.

"That's my sister"

The man smiles.

"You guys don't look alike"

"Yeah, we get that a lot"

I turn around to Nala and raise my eyebrows, we don't normally see guys like that in Brixton. Nala was barely impressed, however.

"You good?"

She shakes her head, grabbing my arm and takes me to the kitchen, turning the microwave on.

"That was the guy that saved me"

Her voice was shaky. I looked at her puzzled but Amen comes in looking like he's gonna beat the crap out of us.

"You guys making food when the ambulance is here seriously?"

He turns off the microwave and see's nothing in it.

"Yeah, you guys have lost it"

He ushers us to the door and the Paramedic looks at us, giving us a big smile.

Nala turns to me, and I shake my head.

"I think I should say something"

"No" I whisper

"Alright Nala you'll be safe in the hospital, police will be there too. Laila you should come with us, I don't want you to be alone"

"What about your dad Amen?" Nala asks.

"My friends gonna stay over"

51

I can't really concentrate on what Amen is saying because the paramedic's eyes start to feel hypnotizing, they feel harsh on mine like there blurring my vision. The room starts to feel too tight for me, to the point where the air felt heavy, and I couldn't breathe in it.

"Laila, you coming?"

They all stare at me confused as I grab on to medics arm for support, my legs completely giving up on me.

"LAILA"

Amen's voice sounded like it came from a mile away but I'm pretty sure he's asking if I'm okay and so are the others. Nala came in front of me and held me up, even when she's blurry she's still so pretty, her brown skin glowing in front of me.

I reach up to touch her perky cheek bones, but my hand never makes it, instead my head starts to feel heavy and begins to fall towards the ground. I hear a loud thump and I wonder where it came from. I can no longer feel most of my body, losing sense of pain feels like I'm transcending but I have no clue where I would transcend to.

I hear screams that become drained out by a small peaceful melody that rings in my ear making me feel slightly calm. My eyes are still wide awake and so is my mouth as I face the blurry ceiling. Amen and Nala's faces popping right on top of me, their heads look like their floating.

"Laila your gonna be okay"

A panic voice says blocking the peaceful music that surrounds my ears.

I feel a liquid surrounding my mouth that makes my mouth feel numb, unable to move.

I don't know what's more ironic, the fact that I could die before baba or that I'm relishing this feeling of being close to death. The idea of going to the other side always intrigued me but as I look around, amens blurred face comes into view and a sudden wave of guilt punches me right in the gut.

I can feel myself lifted of the ground by Amen and before I'm carried outside the door, my head moves on its own uncontrollably and I make eye contact with baba on the sofa. His eyes are the only thing I can clearly see in a room filled with blurred faces. His eyes open wide staring deep into mine, I haven't seen them that open since mama's death, and I wonder if he wants to say something to me but can't. As soon as they open however, they shut abruptly and I'm outside the house surrounded in cold air. I can see bright red and blue lights in the sky. Loud voices coming from several people but one I'm concentrated on, is Amens. The words coming out his mouth sound so foreign to me as he lays me down on a hard surface and holds my hand tightly.

A mask goes on my face allowing me to finally breath, but it soon becomes my last breath as black spots surround my eyes and I close them accepting the darkness graciously.

I don't know how much time has passed but when I wake up, I'm lying in a hospital bed with white bright lights that are nearly blinding.

Amen and Nala in the other side of the room talking to two police officers in my line of vision. They look too stressed and busy talking to them to notice me, Amen covers his face with his hands and nala hugs him tightly.

He looks so broken that I feel bad for enjoying the darkness without him.

I sit up on the hospital bed and adjust my eyes to the light, the sound of nurses rushing around waking me up bit by bit and the smell of coffee fanning my nostrils makes my eyes shoot up to the ceiling.

   "Water" I sputter out.

Everyone stops talking for a second, stopping everything that they're doing and looks at me. The nurses and the handsome doctor on the other side of the room look at me with wide eyes and Nala's mouth hanging open.

   "LAILA"

She runs at me and squeezes me in a hug that's impossible to get out off. Her skeletal body deceiving us of her strength. I tap her shoulders so she can let go off me.

"You're awake?" she shouts.

"I think so"

Amen walks over to me with a doctor by his side and two police officers standing by the door but before I can say something my eyes shut close without my permission. My body begins to shake on its own and Amen's familiar yelling is heard throughout the room. My body was moving without my consent, violently thrashing around the bed.

In a brief moment the man's face comes to my mind, he had a scar on his left eye that digs deep into the surface of his sun burnt skin. When he saw me, his eyes had penetrated mine and haunted the deepest part of my consciousness that resides all my buried secrets.

The blood that dripped through his mouth as he feasted on what felt like my neck sparked an unspoken wound inside me, an emotion I've never felt even when my mother died. A painful abandonment and forsaken pain that felt overwhelmingly menacing. Seeing him look at me terrified me and yet aroused me but I was unable to move or speak to him.

It was far too real to have been a hallucination and as my ears try to focus on what everyone was saying, I'm sucked back into the darkness of his eyes. I'm consumed by his face and plagued by his demonic punctured eye that laced itself with lust.

I look down at my feet to try and shake of the images of him and I begin to switch my focus on to my bland grey socks which are covered in wet spots. As I keep staring at them, more wet droplets form on my feet.

I notice there coming from my hijab. I look at Nala who hasn't seemed to notice as she just eyes the paramedic.

I was back in my living room, re living the moments before I fainted.

 Didn't this already happen? This time it feels much different.

I grab my neck; my scarf was soaking with blood.

Strangely enough I want to smile because for once I don't feel crazy.

Wouldn't this be proof that Noah did dig his teeth into my neck. That man was dangerously close to eating me whole.

   "Are you ok babe? Nala asks.

She looks at me, concern etched in her features, as she turns her attention to the hand on my neck covering my blood.

I look into her eyes and slowly remove my hand which is painted in a light red colour, and I willingly watch as her eyes expand in shock.

She screams so loud that I grab my ears and cover them. Her scream still ringing my ears painfully.

Her eyebrows dug deep into her forehead almost leaving a dent.

At this point in time everything moves in slow motion, Nalas hands moving towards the skin of my neck, and I don't stop her letting her see the beautiful proof of my story.

She feels the blood that was meant to be on hers, and we both look at the two marks spread apart at the end of my neck where it meets my shoulder.

   "It's exactly like"

She pauses, her eyes meeting mine and in a brief moment she looks at me with fear as if she were re living what she went through tonight, her expression painted beautifully on her face.

A black shadow slowly makes it way over her though and the living room becomes dimmer than usual to the point where I have to squint to see everyone.

I can barely here the words coming out of Nalas mouth. The quiet feels deadly and not something one would like to stay in but one I would gladly stay in to keep me protected from what might come. I can feel my neck squirting out blood like it was a hose.

I'm suddenly floating in a black hole, and I feel like I'm going to fall in deaths arms any second now, but some sort of string is driving me back to the physical world and I can't shake of the dreadful thought of it having to do with what I saw through that mirror.

I can hear Nala and Amen shouting my name.

"What did you do? Amen's yelling begin to sound like faint distorted whispers.

Me? I couldn't have done this but seeing my previous history with digging holes into my skin he wouldn't expect anything less of me.

"Get the bed" Amen shouts at the paramedics.

All I focus on is the blood on my hand. It looks fake like it doesn't belong to me, but I know it can only be mine because its coming out of me, it just doesn't look the way it always does.

Whenever I'd see my blood through other deadly practises it was always much darker, this however looked like it had come from a Halloween shop.

This was definitely not mine but before I could speak my thoughts Amen picks me up swiftly in his arms, moving me towards the door. The paramedics rushing to open the bed for me.

Just before Amen reaches the outdoors, I see baba again in the couch, his head lifted looking at me with his eyes wide again.

He mouths something but I can't hear, and I doubt anyone can with Amen and Nalas hysterical cries. I send him an empty smile, his face resembling one that's seen a devil and I wonder if it's the last time he will look at me like that. Bedridden and almost soulless, baba doesn't look at me for more than a second nor does he speak. His eyes are almost pleading with me but as soon as our eyes meet, they're quickly ripped apart as I'm escorted outside to the fresh cold London air.

I'm ushered inside the ambulance leaving him inside alone in the empty house stained with the smell of blood. I can faintly see our nosy neighbours outside of their houses, their faces abit blurred to me but nonetheless their figures stand watching the entertainment of the week slide through an ambulance.

"You're going to be okay" A unfamiliar voice says. My upper right arm is wrapped tightly in a band as the doors shut, closing the coldness away from me.

The lights inside the ambulance are rapidly digging holes into my eyes. It feels like how I would imagine lava to feel if it touched ones skin instead it's touching my eyes. I shut them close feeling the darkness to be safer than the torture of those lights.

"LAILA"

That was Amen, but I can't really respond to him as a familiar foamy liquid starts to surround my mouth, making it difficult to even breath or move. I don't know what's more ironic, the fact that I could die before my dad or that I'm relishing in the feeling of being close to death once again. The idea of going to the other side always intrigued me ever since I started puberty.

Something makes its way on to my face allowing me to breath, but it soon becomes my last breath as black spots surround my eyes and I admire them accepting the inevitable.

Oxygen seems like the least of my concerns, and I almost don't remember the action of breathing as everything feels so still. My entire body is suddenly on hold.

In the midst of the darkness everything becomes so piercingly silent. I find myself in a cold room with no furniture.

On the walls of this room are biblical scriptures thinly carved onto the walls. The wall in front of me however are filled with drawings like they were done with someone's nails.

I walk closer to it, and I see faces of people screaming and crying and right in the centre I see Nala. She's drawn with her mouth hanging open and her eyes closed in pain as she extends her neck to the left, her curly hair is sticking to her face, exactly like it was when she came to us tonight.

I reach my hand out to touch her drawing, but I instantly hear footstep creeping up behind me, and I turn around, the room transforming into one with furniture.

A mattress lies in the corner of the room to my left and creepily enough human heads are hanged up on each wall except the wall with the drawings. The biblical scriptures are in bold. 'Thou shall not kill' imbedded on a women's forehead, her eyes where wide open like she's seen a ghost. The human heads surrounding her mimicked her expression.

A door emerges in the other end of the room. It slowly begins to open and a bald man steps in. He checks the room, looking at the masterpiece of heads with a frown.

"It's empty" he says.

He definitely can't see me because this room is small, and I felt huge inside it.

A man with blood gushing out of his mouth follows him from behind, he was crippled with eyes swollen and an ear missing. The bald man reminds me of the paramedic but this one wears a kippa on his head and has two curls on the side of his face, the exact description Nala described the man that saved her.

He wore jeans that were slightly baggy on his tall slim figure, and he wore a stained navy-blue sweater with a white undershirt. He looked like he hadn't showered in weeks. His eyes landed on mine for a brief second and then went back to the man behind him.

"That's the girl?" he points to me.
I thought they couldn't see me? like the ceremony I went unnoticed.
My hands begin to shake uncontrollably as they walk towards me.
The man with a destroyed face shakes his head as I hold my breath, my heart beating so loud, I'm sure they could even hear it.
"She's just the friend remember, you saw her"
He says in between coughs of blood.
The bald man slumps his shoulders.
"Yeah, I was referring to the friend. Idiot"
He was so close to me that I could see his features in the light so clearly. He was the same man that came to the house. He looked much different, but his features were the same. I can hear more footsteps that sound like their coming up some stairs.
I carefully move to my right treading quietly to remain invisible, but the floorboard has other plans and gives me away with a loud long irritating screech.
"What was that?"
They turned around the room and frowned.
"Do jinn's stay here?"
"Som...sometimes"
"What kind of Jinn's?"
"Don't worry only the good kind, they won't rat you out"
They look at the space I was in, and the bald guy moves to the picture of Nala thankfully not spotting me.
He frowns when he's a few feet away from her drawing.
I'm close to him but not close enough where he can reach me, but I can see the side of his face, his skin so sickly pale.
His eyebrows knit together, and he opens his left hand, and his nails extend effortlessly. He scrapes his nails over her face. The screeching sound makes my skin crawl. The man

behind him grabs a knife out of his pocket and slowly moves closer to the bald guy.

I don't know what came over me, but I instinctively move to protect him without realising but someone else grabs him by his neck. A man even I didn't notice was already holding him up from the neck, nearly choking him.

"Rule number 1, don't turn your back on a fugitive" Noah. His voice was warm and yet void of any emotion. He was in the same clothes from when I saw him last. So utterly captivating in his black uniform. His robe was tied on his waist however as his tight black shirt covered most of him.

He throws the guy in the corner of the room as if he weighed nothing.

He collides with one of the heads on display and grunts in pain, more blood rushing out of his mouth. He only has one long fang.

The bald guy closest to me doesn't move a muscle, he just observes Nalas face on the wall not turning around to Noah.

"I just did that to test you, you know if you have my back"

He turns around to wink at Noah to which he just rolls his eyes and looks around the room with disgust.

"What is this place?"

They look over at the beaten guy.

"Why did you bring us here?"

The bald guy makes the man sit up straight.

Noah opens his hand, and a ball of fire comes out it.

I clasp my hand over my mouth trying not to gasp aloud. The fire lights the room and his face. I couldn't forget his face but, in the light, it was even clearer than the ceremony where the fire from Iblis was the only source of real light. His scar tunnelling through his left eye to his chin. His face is less threatening now than it was when I saw him last.

He looked like he could eat you alive and then thank you for your sacrifice but now he looks normal almost human. As normal as one could be creating a fire through his hand something only fictional characters could do.

"This is where I've been staying trying to find the real Queen"

"So, who's that?"

"Her friend like he said twice already" the bald guy interrupts.

"Alright Uri what's with the attitude"

I didn't expect his name to be Uri, but it suited him so well.

"Well, you've been out of it the whole journey here"

"Um yeah maybe that's because theirs random people looking for my mate, that I haven't even met yet"

He pushes him out of the way. His presence so hostile. He puts his flame to Nala's face.

"Where she from?"

They look at the beaten man, who's grabbing on to his jaw.

"She's Somalian, she lives in London"

"Yeah, we know she lives in London, dimwit" Uri sighs.

"But prophecy doesn't mention she would be in London but that she would come from Northern Africa specifically the Desert"

"How do you know about this prophecy and who else knows?"

They have to be talking about me, I'm Nala's only friend. What's unsettling is I don't know why. What could possibly drive them to want to find me.

"The Muslims. Their waiting for her, they've been waiting for her for a while. She's meant to come out now, but she hasn't and their restless."

Uri steps back and looks around the room, he stops right in front of me and sniffs the air.

"You guys smell that?"

I look up at him his beard reaching my head.

"Yeah, Smells like blood in here"

"It's foul" the beaten man says.

Noah and Uri shake their heads.

"Not foul just intense"

Uri agrees.

I touch my neck; it was still leaking with blood. I try to hold it tightly, so it doesn't leak but unfortunately a droplet of blood escapes my hand and lands on the floor. The noise of the drop was so loud creating a stain in the air.

All three of the men swing their heads to the blood and exactly like I saw through my bathroom mirror, their fangs extend out of their mouths.

They were so long it nearly touched their chins. It was like they were humans one minute and beasts the next. Noah looks at Uri who looks like he's about to explode out of his body.

"URI" Noah yells.

Uri turns to Noah and bares his fangs at him. His face looks like a wild animal about to hunt.

Everything happens too quickly for my brain to manage but in no time, Noah is grabbing Uri down to the floor and Uri is thrashing around in his grip. His teeth are snapping at Noah and the veins on his face are turning black quickly consuming him.

The Beaten man sees them fighting and begins to stand up, making a run for it out the door. They don't seem to notice him and slowly their fading away from me and their yelling is becoming inaudible.

Chapter four ~ Uri is here.

Going back to the silence of emptiness was so soothing. The yelling stopped and I was finally comfortable in my physical body.

I open my eyes ever so slowly, making sure I'm not back in that room with them.

Thankfully, I'm surrounded with a bliss silence and hushed whispers and not to mention I'm lying in a comfortable bed where my back sinks deep into the mattress.

My eyes are only half open because the lights here are too bright.

Three police officers have a heated discussion with Amen in the corner of the room by the door. There was noise everywhere, but it was diluted as I focus on Nala's.

A female officer talks to Nala who's sitting close to me on a grey beaten up sofa. She has a notepad out as she asks Nala some questions.

"What time would you say the attack happened"

Nala puts her hands through her hair and huffs.

"Well, I get off work at 9 so maybe 9:30?"

"It takes you that long to walk to your friend's house from McDonald's?"

"Like I said to the others I took a detour"

I can tell when Nala is pissed off and right now, she's one more question away from exploding.

The women's tone was condescending. She looks at Nala with a hint of pity and disbelief as she clicks her tongue and takes notes on her pad.

Amen on the other hand puts his hands over his hair and shuts his eyes closed bombarded with frustration and anger. He does that before every mental breakdown.

I haven't seen him this way since mama died and frankly, I don't want to. I can feel his stress on my shoulders.

I open my mouth to say his name, but it doesn't move.

I hesitate before I try again his name coming out of my mouth this time, but no one hears me. I try to say it louder but still, it was as if I didn't exist. It's like I'm always not existing now a days.

I try to wave or lift any muscle in my body, and I fail, utterly paralyzed to this bed. I want to scream so bad, but my eyes are the only thing I can move so I blink countlessly until tears well up in my eyes and their draining my cheeks.

No one notices me again, but a man walks into the room, I notice him right away. It was Uri. He wasn't dressed like a paramedic anymore, but he looks exactly like I last saw him but this time he wasn't having a meltdown over my blood.

I don't know what I've done to deserve this but once I've woken up from this nightmare, I'm going to pray every day until I die and never commit a speck of sin until I'm on the other side.

He looks around him, no one seems to notice or acknowledge his presence, so he walks all the way up to my bed and stares down at me.

His skin was so smooth underneath his beard that took up most of his face, the only thing that stands out to me was his eyes.

He looks much cleaner than I just saw him a few seconds ago. His face was dirt free, and he smelled good too like a minty bar of soap.

It was like he was familiar like someone you dreamt about, an unknown face you made up but suddenly coming to life. I could still be in the dream world right now, but I wish I weren't, I was tired of seeing things and being unseen. I just want these visions to end.

He didn't move or say anything, but he kept creepily staring me down with his skinny tall frame.

He wasn't the stereotype model of attractive, but he could be the stereotype model of a depressed twenty something man on the verge of going to his tenth night in a row without sleep.

I raise my eyebrows at him, and he did the same copying me.

What a cunt.

I'm sure he knows I can't speak, stupid tall bald cunt. He finally gives up his staring game and bends over close to my ear.

"You alright Love?"

His British accent much stronger now.

He takes of my oxygen mask and the air is sucked out of me. My eyes shake in disbelief at his actions. Is he trying to kill me?

I try to move my body to get the mask, but my body feels like a brick wall so utterly stuck to this bed.

I need the mask it was only way for me to breath. He smiles as he watches me beg for it with my eyes.

I give him a pleading look but he's way to close for comfort, so I look the other way and try to get Amens attention but to no avail.

He holds the oxygen mask and sways it between me and him, teasingly. No one can even see me struggling.

"You only think you can't breathe Laila; your mind is deceiving you"

His voice was so soft and quiet.

"If you just imagine yourself breathing, you won't need this stupid thing"

I do as he says, desperately fighting for my life and imagine myself breathing. The air going in and out and soon as I was actually breathing, feeling the breath dancing all over my lungs.

Uri nods his head surprised at how quick that took me.

"Well, that was easy, wasn't it?"

I breath so loud that I can't even hear what he's saying.

"Can you back away?" I gasp.

Surprised at my own voice I let out a cough following several others as he just smirks at me, my bed supporting his body. He looks around the room again and then at his watch.

"Listen Laila I-"

"How do you know my name"

"Really? That's your first concern?"

From everything that happened tonight I'm not surprised at him knowing my name but more relieved that this wasn't all a dream.

"What you saw tonight"

He looks at the police officers next to Amen on the other side of the room.

"You can't tell them" he says leaning on my bed.

"Why can't I?"

I pause remembering Noah when he dug his teeth inside me. He looked devasted doing so and almost repulsed by me.

"Those marks are gone" he whispers into my ear.

I try to move my hand to my neck, and it works, my arm actually moving. It's feels like it weighs a building but at least it moves.

I touch my smooth bare neck with no trace of a bite.

"Where did it go?"

"You healed yourself Laila"

"How?"

He sighs.

"To be honest we don't know how you actually healed. You're a human"

"Of course, I'm fuckin human"

"Whatever, but you have to stay away from telling them"

"They won't believe me anyway"

"Oh no they will believe you" he smirks.

I glance at him, confused by what he means. My eyebrows furrowed as I bite my lips in agitation.

"You look cute"

"huh?"

He coughs and shakes his head.

"They'll believe you enough to take you away to the Queen"

"Queen Elizabeth?"

He laughs at me, shaking his head

"No ha…Your funny but they'll take you straight to The Vampire queen. For now, I don't want that happening to you"

"Wait Vampire?"

He looks at me with an ominous look.

"Yeah, everything you saw tonight, didn't that remind you of I don't know…vampires?"

I nod. He was right they were the exact description. I couldn't deny it any longer.

"I just never heard it out loud before"

"I saw you in the room tonight, how are you able to stay hidden and spy on us"

I shrug my shoulders. I still don't even know how. I look over at Nala she was staring at me blankly.

"Why was that man after Nala, why was her face on that wall?"

"Long story but your friend isn't the one he's after"

I don't want to hear what he has to say because it could be me and I wasn't ready to know why.

"Yeah, he wasn't meant to find you guys, but now things have changed"

I hesitate before asking.

"What has changed?"

He smiles up at me.

"What changed?" I persist.

He looks away and fiddles with a bracelet in his hand.

"Never mind what Laila it's all about why" he says with a sly smile on his face.

I give him a dead pan look.

"Why then?"

"Soon they'll announce a new kingdom in Jerusalem."

"That's-"

"Crazy?"

I nod my head.

"So, what does that have to do with me?"

His smile drops and he takes of the bracelet he's wearing.

"Let's just say your prophesised to destroy Jerusalem and some don't want it to be destroyed"

I pause before blurting out a laugh.

"What in the hell are you blabbering on about, Jerusalem?"

"I'm blabbering on about you destroying the future Kingdom of Jerusalem"

I can't help but let out another laugh. Not that it should be funny, but I can't help it.

"Yeah, you can laugh now"

He begins to laugh with me and then I notice that no one still detects us.

"How come they can't see you"

"They can't see you either, all they see is your physical body asleep on the bed. You can create the illusion of them seeing what you want the humans to see whilst also communicating with those in the spiritual world"

I look at him, confused.

"You need to wear this; it will stop you from seeing things you shouldn't."

"So, I'm in the spiritual world right now?"

He hums a yes and grabs my hand to put the bracelet on and I gasp. He quickly lets go.

"Sorry"

"Your hand its"

"Cold?"

I nod my head looking at him disgusted.

His hand felt like I was touching my freezer, and you could see the veins popping out it.

He puts the bracelet on ignoring me, his face turning sour like mine as he sees my expression.

He turns to leave but I grab his hand again no matter how cold it is. He turns around to look at me and raises his eyebrows.

"What if I don't want them to stop?"

His face drops in a deadly expression, he leaned into me like he was on the verge to kill me. I felt so alive at the possibility of death once again. Something was disgustingly wrong with me and judging from his face I know he could sense it. My eyes were seducing him to make the next move all on their own.

"Laila"

He touches my cheek making sure to cover his cold hand with his sleeve.

"You can't be caught"

I move his hand from my face, physical contact isn't my forte. His words though punching me deep in my gut. How dare this stranger look at me with pleading eyes.

"Why do you care?"

"Your entire existence Laila is more important than you think but for now you have to keep wearing that if you want Nala or your brother safe"

His voice is unwavering making him so irresistibly believable.

"Will I see him again?"

He fakes a smile and at this point I can't count how many times he's done that.

I'm not sure how I feel about him, but I know I enjoyed it when Noah bit into me.

"Uri"

He looks at me like one looks at a child and I feel even more inferior to him than I do any adult.

He fluffs my pillow and sighs.

"Don't say my name again"

He steps away from me.

"Keep that on"

"What. That's it?"

"Oh, and a doctor will come to take your blood, make sure he takes it from your right hand where the bracelet is"

"Why?"

He doesn't respond but just rushes to walk away from me and turns his back to me once he's at the door and gives me a wave.

"What a Cunt"

He closes the door and suddenly everyone in the room is looking at me.

"Watch your language young lady" the nurse says with a scowl drawn on her face.

"Oh my God"

Amen runs over and squeezes me in a tight hug, breathing heavily down my ear.

"Are you okay, how's your head?"

"It's…"

I touch my head.

"Fine I guess"

Nala slowly gets up and walks over to me, the doctor by her side. She has a deep frown etched on her face as she studies me.

"Glad to see your awake"

The doctor says with his deep Irish accent, looking down at me, his hands joined together as if to congratulate me. He had a belly the size of a pregnant women due any day now and he barely has any hair surviving on his head, yet his skin was uncomfortably flawless. I give him a small smile as a thanks.

"Glad to be awake I guess"

"And of course, nothing is wrong with you, we assume you collapsed because of shock of what happened to your friend Nala"

"Shock?"

I look at Amen who looks away from me and so does Nala.

"Well with what happened with your friend here it would have been too overwhelming for anyone we assume that's what made you faint, but your all good now" He says abit too cheery for my liking.

So, Uri was right, I no longer had bite marks in my neck but Amen and Nala witnessed my blood.

"When can she leave?" Amen asks the doctor.

"After we take her blood to run some tests, she can leave" His smile reaches his eye's, and it was unsettling to say the least.

"Which arm would you like to use?" his eyes wide with intrigue.

I wave my right hand, remembering what Uri said. He walks to the other side and pulls up my sleeve. He licks his lips as he looks for my veins.

"Here keep squeezing the ball until I find your vein"

He hands me a ball and as soon I squeeze it, it rips open.

"Shit sorry"

"Don't worry it must have been a flimsy ball, here why don't you squeeze my hand as tight as you can, don't worry it won't rip open" he giggles.

I reach over to his hand and feel his skin. It was as cold as Uri's even colder if that was even possible.

I squeeze his hand tightly not fazed by the coldness anymore. His hand feels like a rock, an icy unbreakable rock. My imagination runs wild as he sticks the needle in my vein and the bag begins to fill with my blood. He could be just like them, and I could be stuck in this circle of hell for a while.

"Your blood is very…bright" he looks at me with a contagious sickly smile.

"Is that normal?" Amen asks.

"Not really no but it's fine nothing to lose sleep over"

I haven't slept well in a few months.

"Police are patrolling our area, Nala is gonna stay with us for the week" Amen says to me.

I look over at Nala who still has a dazed look in her eyes.

   "Does your dad know?" I ask.

She nods her head without looking at me.

She's not normally this quiet, even when she was attacked, she was still loud, I wonder what happened to her once innocent face.

   "What time is it?"

Amen and Nala look at each other.

   "It's 4am"

  "I was out a while huh?"

They nod their heads and look at me as if my head were about to burst open, and they'd be drenched with blood and the remains of my brain.

   "Can you get me a coffee" Nala asks Amen.

  "Yeah sure"

Nala watches him walk out and as he closes the door, leaving us alone as eventually everyone else begins to leave too.

   "I saw him"

Nala looks behind her as the last police officer leaves through the door.

   "Saw who?"

I fiddle with my covers and so does Nala as she sits on my bed.

   "That man the same one that saved me"

   "You did? I thought no could see him"

Nala gets up and looks outside the door window.

"Why was he here?"

I sit up on my bed. I can hear her heart beating as if it was right next to me on my ear.

"I- I feel like I'm going crazy Laila"

She turns around to me and grabs her head.

"It's like theirs voices in my head"

I don't know what she means but I feel like I'm going crazy too, her face was on that wall amongst many others, and I can't seem to unsee it.

"What are the voices like?"

She walks towards me, her eyes wide with no sleep.

"Like people crying...I think, I don't know, it's confusing"

The room had other faces in it that all looked like they were screaming.

"Nala, I think I know why"

"Why?"

As I go to tell her Amen walks in with our coffee.

"What'd I miss?"

Amen looks at our faces, with no hint of a smile and immediately puts his hands up.

"That was fast?" Nala says.

"Yeah, the machine's only down the hall"

He hands Nala the coffee to which she takes and gulps it all down.

"Yo, take it easy your gonna burn yourself"

Nala keeps on going though until not one last drop of coffee is left. She wipes her mouth.

"More"

She hands Amen the cup.

Amen looks at it and chuckles but not in an amused way.

"Okay...okay"

He throws the coffee in the trash, aiming perfectly at it and then puts his hands on his hips and looks at us both like he's, our parent. Frankly, I'd normally be intimated but right now I'm just tired and confused and I think Nala is too.

"Can you girls just tell me what happened today"
We both don't respond.

"Please, both of you are acting weird and not like your normal weird. Believe it or not I actually care about you both. So, if there's something going on you should tell me now because I've never seen you guys behave this way…ever."
He's right we should tell him, even if he thinks I'm mental he's still my brother.

"I need to know why you fainted Laila and if you…you did that to yourself"
He points to my neck. He was no longer smiling or walking on eggshells around me.

"I thought you didn't do that anymore"
I close my eyes, ready to hear the lectures again.

"And now on your neck?"
"She didn't" Nala interjects.
She walks over and sits at the end of my bed.

"You know she hasn't for a while Amen"
"So then how, she was by herself in there"
She looks at me as if to say I should just tell him.

"I…I ummm" I fidget with my sleeves.
"Your right, I was alone" I breath.
Nala and Amen look at me confused.

"You threw out anything I could use to harm myself with remember?"
Amen nods.

"There's nothing I have anymore that can do something like this" I point to my neck

"So how then" Amen asks.

"I saw something in the mirror" I told him in Arabic.
When I speak in the mother tongue, it always feels more serious.

74

"Wallah, I won't lie about this ever"
My breaths are shaky as I explain to him everything I saw through the mirror, and he listens without interrupting.
Nala puts her head down on her hands as I finish explaining to him what happened, and she huffs loudly.

"Fuck they're still in my head"
Amen still as a statute still trying to process everything I said turns to Nala.

"Who's in your head" Amen asks.

"I don't know, it like someone's saying something but it's just coming out as cries"

"You're both seeing and hearing things, so you've both gone mad, or this is just some joke to you. Am I a joke to you?"
He sits down on the sofa and rubs his temple.

"I know how it sounds" I say.

"No, you fucking don't. When the police question you both today, you know how dumb your gonna sound? How am I gonna explain this to my team? How am I gonna explain that my own sister is making up shit like vampires"
I sit up on my bed facing him as I throw the bed sheets off from my body.

"I haven't lied to you in a long time Amen"
I answer seriously.
I can feel a tear coming out of my eye.

"I saw something else when I passed out. I was in this room, and I saw Nalas face was carved on the wall, the paramedic guy from today was there with that same guy that bit into my neck from the mirror, and they were looking for someone"

"Do you even hear yourself Laila?"
"The paramedic guy he came in here, Nala you saw him, right? He was real"
Amen turns to Nala his eyebrows raised.

"I did see him Amen, he was like a ghost, nobody else noticed him"

"But you noticed him?"

Nala nods.

"So, your saying this guy that was also the paramedic came in to chat with you and he was the same one you saw in this strange room that had her face on it and that this guy was with Noah the man that supposedly hurt you?

"Well, it didn't actually hurt" I mumbled.

"Yeah, you know what that was a nice convincing story Laila but the paramedic's that got you tonight were all women including the driver. So, I suggest both of you come up with a better lie to tell me"

He looks like such a parent I almost forgot what he even said. All women?

"What? They were all women?" I ask.

"No Amen you don't understand, we both saw a man the same man we didn't just fucking make him up, he was the same one that saved me from the man that attacked me. What are you gonna say I made that up too?"

Nala is beyond frustrated right now her nose expanding as she shoots daggers at him.

"Nala I'm trying my best to believe you but when your both making this fairy-tale shit up, I'm finding it hard to. There were no men tonight"

"Can you at least check CCTV; he was in the room before you realised, she woke up. I saw it with my own eyes."

"So why didn't you say anything?"

"I couldn't even move once I saw him"

Amen sighs and clicks his tongue.

"I'm gonna go and check the cameras in the hospital just to entertain your fantasies for now but when the police come to question you...just say you don't remember anything. If you start telling them this shit your gonna end up in trouble"

He gets up and leaves the room, slamming the door behind him without looking at us.

"I shouldn't have told him"
I look at Nala.

"Maybe, but if he sees him on camera then he's got to believe us, right?"
I shake my head; my anxiety really getting the best of me at this point.
Why do I feel like Uri won't be on camera? He looked like a ghost as Nala said and he's a vampire. One thing for sure though is we both can see him which gives me abit of comfort that I'm not making things up.

"He said there was no man as a paramedic, so if we were the only ones that saw him, then what makes you think the camera's will?"

"Shit"

"Yeah, shit. I should have just said I did it to myself"

"But you haven't, you shouldn't have to lie"

"But at least he won't think I'm a liar"

"It's Amen, he's gonna come around I promise"
I don't respond and just take off all the wires attached to me.

"Hand me my clothes, I don't want to stay here"

"Laila are you crazy, theirs police everywhere waiting for us outside"

"I don't care Nal, I'm leaving!"

Chapter Five ~ Masih's Kingdom.

The sun began to rise in the east, it's fiery colours painting over the darkness and shadows of the island. The birds set out to sing in a system of ecstasy to disrupt every creature who's sound asleep in this quiet hollow place. The trees follow suit and hum in a serene remedy on the island, which was near the middle east, but it wasn't on any world map. Situated far from humans eyes and hidden by The Vampire kingdom so only those that are allowed in can find it.

Those that know off it don't bother to find it unless invited because of what lives in it.

The island has become a safe haven for the vampires, hidden from all humans apart from the ones that can see beyond what the human eye lets them.

It can only welcome the supernatural and repel those that are out to destroy it, because God has created this place for the beast who has been chained right in the centre of it's beautiful maze.

When one travels further away from the beast, they can find a gothic temple situated in a cocoon of trees. It rings its bells every morning at fajir before the sunrises like today. So, the vampires can stay hidden from the sun.

Male vampires with black robes that reach their ankles fall from the sky and land effortlessly on the ground. About three hundred men appear from the sky all dressed modestly and not an ounce of joy on each of their faces. There was nothing joyful about the sunrising and the night ending to them.

Only some of the Elite Vampires could come enter this temple and those were the Hanesh and Abesh clan.

They had extravagant long straight hair sleeked back form their faces. They each carry their own hair colour to differentiate them between their clan.

The Hanesh had platinum blond hair and they are the first rank in the kingdom whilst the brunette males are from the Abesh family the second in rank. The Hanesh are physically stronger and closer to the Queens bloodline, but the Abesh are wiser, their brains filled with knowledge that not any vampire can easily acquire.

As they dust off their robes and slick back there hairs with their hands, they walk towards the temple doors.

Each man looks up at the doors and they bow their head and say a prayer in Aramaic before they enter the temple's congregation.

Their words translate to 'death to the chosen one and life to the eternal Beast.'

Women also begin to emerge after all the men walk inside the temple.

The women however come out from the tree's. The tree's in this island were portals to humans. When they wanted fresh human blood and were burning to hunt them down like a sick game, they used the tree's in the island to quickly travel to them.

Their face's so pale you wouldn't think they'd belong in the middle east underneath the scorching sun.

The Abesh women giving way for the Hanesh to go inside first.

They all carried themselves with class and dignity. Their beauty cutting through the misery in this island.

They all carry a serious expression on their faces, any that human who saw them today would prefer to end their own life instead of being seen by them.

Today's congregation was unusual however, the Vampires were gathering for a meeting held by the Queen which doesn't usually happen.

They all wait for the Queen, some more on the edge than the others.

Inside the temple it was twice as large as it looked from the outside. There were seats for only the Women whilst the men stand by the walls each clan on either side, none of them dare to mix with the other. There was a mutual respect for each other, but they would rather not interact so closely, preferring their boundaries.

A group of elders in the council emerge in the centre stage of the temple. It was lit with candles as the elders arrive from underneath the temple through a door that leads to the underworld where many creatures live.

They dust of their robes and take their seats. There were eight male and two female elders, which advised the Queen.

They all cover their noses with their robes as the temple was filled with jinn's but the unclean kind, the ones that liked to bathe in dirt and manure of animals. When one opens the doors for the underground, many jinn's escape it. That was the downside of living underground.

One of the elders stands up from his chair as the Queen arrives.

"Sisters you may start" an elder addresses the women. The women begin to sing a prayer, it's melody mixed with their serene voices create a calming sound of peace even the Jinn's swayed to the song with their mouths open.

This song creates a protection on the temple, keeping out the Angels from ever entering it. Jinn's can gather outside the temple without worry.

They are unseen creatures that travel between the physical and spiritual world but Some of them are among the good that are servants of God, but most are now captured slaves of the vampire Kingdom and are forced to do as the Queen commands.

They mostly carry out the vampires dirty work, like drag the dead bodies to the temples to be feasted upon and lure innocent humans into the woods.

The candles begin to float in the air as the Queen body emerges from a portal.

The Queen of the Anesh and the mother of Vampire's walks through the portal and immediately everyone falls silent and stands for the Queen bowing their heads in respect. Throughout history it has been told that the queen birthed the vampires through Iblis's help.

Whilst the Habesh originate through needed inbreeding from the Arabs that didn't want to follow Gods command and were sent to starve in the dessert all alone until the Queen had saved them and gave them her blood to survive changing them into one of her.

Habesh control the worlds affairs, making sure the humans stay distracted by worldly politics and war. They cause the famine and destruction all in the name of vengeance to the God who banished them.

"You may all sit"

She smiles so gracefully at them. Her blonde hair reaching the floor in simple translucent waves. She has silver eyes with her left eye severely bruised.

Everyone sits as she makes her way over to her throne. She wore a black velvet dress that wrapped around her body and touched the floor.

The temple grows wider as soon as she sits on her chair that is in the centre. The Gold ceilings extend and a serpent statue that was on top of the ceiling becomes alive and slithers across to the Queens lap.

The candles still float on top of her and around the elders creating a mystical environment.

A captivating sight that made one want to sleep.

"I have come here today not to pray for our Lord Iblis but to warn you of what's to come"

~

Outside of the temple, Noah and Uri walk out of the same tree and bend down to the ground. The huge trees cover them from the sun's rays, and they dust of the mud and dirt from their clothes as Noah carries a sample of blood that's labelled, Laila.

"We're late" Uri says as he looks up at the sky.
The sun was in full form. They wouldn't make it to the temple without getting burnt.

"The Queen's gonna have a shit load to say about that" Noah sighs loudly but then he holds up Laila's blood sample.

"But at least we got this" he winks.

"Yeah, getting her blood was so easy, too easy don't ya think?" Uri asks.

Noah shrugs.

"Yeah, Irish people are nice, better than the English" Uri rolls his eyes at him.

"The suns out, you can test it now"
Uri wipes the sweat off his bald head and stares at the bottle. Noah places it to the sun and he hisses in pain as the sun burns his fingers, but it also burns Laila's blood. Her blood moving uncontrollably as if it was alive. He hides back in the shade and puts his hand in the soil relieving him of his pain.

"Arrghhh, I haven't been burnt in ages man"
Uri laughs.

"It doesn't get old mate"

Noah looks at Laila's blood sample. It's still bubbling around the bottle.

"I guess she's not human after all"

"Well, what do you except? Your mate can't be human. Doesn't that like go against the natural order of things"

"But you said you smelt her, and she smelt like a human"

Uri nods his head.

"Yeah, she definitely did. But he did say she had a spell on her, so maybe that's what she wanted me to smell"

"I've never seen a spell that can do that. We have to look into her mother"

"Yeah, you can't really find much with a dead person"

Noah smirks.

"Well one things for sure is the Queen's not going to like that I have a mate"

Uri scoffs and takes of his kippa on his head. No religious items where allowed inside the temple.

"Are you ready to tell the Queen? Are you sure you can handle it"?

"I can handle anything Uri"

"Even if she asks you to ki-"

"Yes Uri, I'll do whatever it takes to be King"

Uri goes silent, he realises how much it means to Noah, but the Queen can be ruthless. A soul mate is someone attached to you, someone you can't run away from. Even if your soulmate was trapped under a mountain, they will still find you. A sacrifice this big can hurt anyone, even Noah.

Uri turns to look at the temple. The sun was glaring daggers at them making them sweat buckets.

"knowing the Queen, she probably already has her dogs searching for her since the ceremony. She's not a fool ya know why'd you think she didn't attend last night?"

"I dunno maybe she was constipated. Ya never know"

Uri jokes.

Noah dusts of his jeans and stands up and offers a hand to
Uri which he takes, and he pulls him up from the ground.

"We're not even in uniform"

Noah realises he lost his robe at the man's room.

Uri shakes his head and motions for the door of the temple
that was about a good a mile from them.

"Ready to get burnt?"

"Yeah, fuck it"

"Last one in is a smelly burnt Hanesh"

Noah takes off before Uri can respond and beats him to the
door of the temple out of breath from the heat of the sun.
Their face's and clothes caught in flames.

Uri hisses in pain as his bald head is left with a burn.
They stumble inside the temple in pain dropping to the
ground and patting away their burnt clothes. The doors are
wide open making the vampires hiss as the sun comes in
blinding everyone.

The women and the elders duck underneath the tables to
hide but some get burnt causing chaos inside the temple.
Noah quickly shuts the door, but he ends up dropping
Laila's blood sample. It rolls all the way to the centre, and
It creates a rippling effect between the Vampires, each one
hissing so loudly as they cower away at the jar that rolls
further to where the Queen resides, yet she doesn't show an
inch of emotion to the disturbance of the two men nor the
blood. Her face stoic.

"Sorry your majesty we were caught up with important
business" Uri says.

Uri bows to the Queen and pulls down a frustrated Noah
down with him, but his eyes remain on Laila's blood that
slipped away from his hands.

The Queens silver eyes turn black in the sight of blood and
the Habesh and Anesh cover their noses with their robes to
stop the disastrous smell assaulting their nostrils.

This blood was not human, which is why nobody wanted to
outwardly drink it, instead everyone was repulsed. Some

Abesh were making gagging noises at the smell of it. One women part of the Hanesh looks like she's going to faint from the smell.

The Queens jinn who's attached to her back whispered into her ear whose blood that belonged to.

"Laila" The queen says.

Her black eyes on Noah.

She stands up from her chair and everyone follows, respectfully standing and lowering their heads at her.

"Noah how lovely of you to finally join us"

Noah gets up from his position and looks directly at the queen who is smiling at him.

"Sorry for the late disturbance your majesty"

"That's okay my dear we were waiting for you"

Her eyes glistening at him.

He looked at Uri and coughs.

"So, there is word going around that you have a soulmate. Is this true Noah?"

He looks around the temple. Noah belonged with the Abesh clan. His father was at the front watching him with evil eyes. Glaring at him as if he wasn't even his son.

Everyone else was awaiting the news of the future Kings mate.

"Yes, I have a mate"

Everyone tries to hold in their gasps as Noah holds a stern face whilst saying those words, knowing his responsibilities on finding her would be to inevitably ruin her if he had to mate with Aaliyah.

"Her name is Laila the owner of the blood. And your…mate?"

The queen sits down and so does everyone else. Everyone begins to look at each other and the women steel glances at Aaliyah who was seated in the front row by herself. She was unfazed by the announcement like she's heard it before.

"That's my mates blood"

"And why would you bring it to me?"

Noah walks forward to the centre and reaches for the blood. The Hanesh look at him with jealousy and so do the Anesh men. Noah was picked out of everyone since he was young. He was destined to be King.

"We wanted you to test her blood and see what she is. Me and Uri can only smell her as human, because of a spell"

"What a spell huh?"

The queens face was moving like a doll and so was her voice. Sometimes the Jinn attached to her speaks for her, but her voice still says Gentle like it always is. Only a few vampires have mastered to merge well with their jinn's that they almost go unnoticeable.

Noah nods his head at the Queen.

"It was her mother's spell, but its wearing of because she died"

"How did she die?"

"Um we don't know how"

"Hmm so how do you know she's really dead?"

Uri steps forward.

"She was buried in Algeria year ago, her father is pretty much deceased as well, we checked your majesty"

The Queen clenches her jaw at Uri's interruption.

"Noah, you know the sacrifice you have to do. There will no longer be a mate for you in order to be King. It can and will only be Aaliyah"

"Yes, I know"

"Aaliyah's mate is no longer alive I've made sure of it, Aaliyah killed him in front of me"

Noah looks at Aaliyah, she stares at the floating candles ignoring everyone else.

"So now it's up to you Noah to deal with yours, prove to us you deserve to rule over Jerusalem before tomorrow's mating ceremony"

The Queen spoke so elegantly it was hard not to sway in front of her. Everyone in the Kingdom adored her as their mother but also feared her like an enemy.

"Yes, your majesty I shall bring her to you"

The queen points to the blood.

"And her blood"

She walks over to him and covers her nose.

"You may go to the Masih. He shall know what your mate is. I have never smelt blood like this. It's very…foul"

"It doesn't smell foul to me"

"Well of course not she's your mate"

Noah smiles inside, knowing that her smell only smells nice to him, intoxicating actually. But he also remembers Uri was never repulsed by her blood.

"I give you my blessing to see him"

She pats his shoulder.

"You should have come to me when you first saw her in the ceremony"

Everybody begins to whisper.

Uri takes a step forward.

"We wanted to be sure before we disturbed you, your majesty"

The Queen doesn't acknowledge Uri.

Uri doesn't belong to any clan or family. He was born without a place but worked for Noah's family as a teen boy and then adopted by them when he turned eighteen.

However, the queen did not allow him to be a Habesh because biologically he wasn't, so he became an outsider that didn't belong here in the queens eye and everyone else agreed but didn't say anything because of Noah.

"You may go to the Beast now and show him the blood, make sure you don't let him play too many tricks on you"

The Queen lifts her hand and a Hanesh man drags out two African vampires.

"You may drink from them to walk in the sun. My jinn's will lead you straight to him and after your done join us underneath"

Noah and Uri bow their heads in front of the Queen. Everyone watches them walk forward to the captured African Vampires. Their hair masking most of their faces, but their bright red eyes shine through their hair.

"Extend your neck"

They extend their necks to Noah and Uri to drink from them.

They were both Sudanese, one of them was a women and another a man, only melanated vampires could have access to walk in the sun. They were never cursed as the white Vampires were. They obeyed God and were the first to do so when Moses came to them and told them the way of the Lord. However, the Queen enslaved them because of her jealousy and greed.

Noah and Uri wipe their mouth clean as their body pumps with a rush of adrenaline and newfound power. The Sudanese vampires were under a spell they couldn't move or speak.

"We will go to Him now your majesty" Noah says with his head bent down.

The blood from the vampires making him lose ability to think clearly as the power of their blood takes it course.

They walk steadily out of the temple everyone watches their every move.

Uri opens the door for Noah to follow out and they finally see the sun. Their greatest enemy and threat to their existence.

The biggest challenge is to capture an African Vampire as their too agile and clever for them to capture. Their security is one of a kind and at the moment the Queen only has two left who she captured two hundred years ago.

One of them broke out of the spell and tried to escape a year ago but failed due to being weak from having their blood drank every day by the Queen, and so he wasn't able to run long enough before he gave up.

The vampires in Somalia and Ethiopia are particularly wickeder than any African breed of vampires. No one dares to step foot on their land, not even the Queen herself as their ability to hide and de track their scent makes them feared across the globe. No one knows where they hide or if their waiting to devour their enemy.

Even the Jinn's refuse to help.

The vampires in the African desert are especially harder to capture as they can hide inside the sand when any vampire from the Kingdom comes to catch them.

The only way the Queen could lure these two was through her charms, an old spell that made them think she was human. They fell for her lies and her innocent looking face and she quickly had the Hanesh capture them at night. The Africans know never to trust anyone ever again in case it's another spell.

"We need to hurry before their blood stops working on us"

Noah says to an anxious Uri on his left. Uri looks like he's drunk, his eyes trying to adjust to this kind of blood rushing through his veins.

"I've never drank from them before I feel-"

"Alive?"

"Yeah"

"I have and it never gets old, to walk in the sun"

Uri shakes his head as his eyes are wide with adrenaline. He rolls his sweater and sees his veins moving and bulging out of his skin.

He stares up at the sun.

"I was always jealous you got to walk out during the day when we were young"

"Well, I had to do those stupid appearances, so the Government thinks I'm human"

"How long does it wear out?"

"A few hours, there blood used to last days but their getting weaker. The Queen gave dad and his soldiers orders to set up camp in Morocco. They need new slaves, and she wants them from the desert"

The Jinn's start to disappear in front of them, but their footsteps can be seen imprinted on the ground.

"Well lets hurry before we get burnt"

The Jinn's pick up their pace and begin to run ahead. The Beast lives up a steep mountain, one wrong move and you'll fall to your death, but they were already dead.

Noah turns behind him as he looks down at the temple that begins to be sucked into the ground, in its place a tree begins to grow, leaving no evidence of the temple's existence.

"Come on mate"

Uri pulls Noah's hand.

As they hike up. the sun begins to blind them.

"When you see him, don't look at him for more than a second and make sure not to speak even if he wants you to"

With a confused look Uri looks to Noah.

"Why?"

"Remember I'm a Hanesh and you're not"

Uri looks away.

"Right."

"Don't take it personal but if the Jinn's tell the Queen you communicated with him, she'd really kick you out then"

"And feed my soul to em"

He nods to the Jinn's in front of him.

Noah elbows Uri and mouths 'don't.'

Uri shakes his head and grumbles in annoyance but all of a sudden, the Jinn's stop walking their footprints show them running the opposite direction.

"We're here brother" Noah says.

Noah steps Infront of Uri and shields him from the light escaping the trees. The trees bend away and create room for them to pass by.

"Don't close your eyes no matter how much you want to, he's testing us" Noah says.

"You're practically shielding me from it you cunt"
"He can manipulate light energy and make you see it even brighter" Noah whispers.

As they walk through the pathway, Noah keeps his eyes wide, not an inch of him looks as though he would give up. Then the light swiftly starts to fade and around them is an empty green space on top of the mountain. Below them they could see the ocean and trees that look so minuscule. There was absolute silence surrounding this area, that the only sound they can hear is their heavy breathing.

"He's waiting for you"

A centaur emerges out in front of them which startles Uri but not Noah. His face is as still as the air around them. The centaur has hair all the way down to his feet and his lower body was of a white silky horse.

He points to the cave behind him.

"He's inside"

They walk inside the cave Uri still behind Noah's protection as he looks at the creepy centaur that was too beautiful to be male, Uri thought.

Inside the cave, it was dark even for them to see. The smell in the air was no longer there, it was like an empty whole where nothing existed. Uri looks behind him as the entrance of the cave begins to close. He taps Noah's shoulder, but Noah doesn't turn around or acknowledges him, completely shifting to someone unrecognisable.

They enter the centre of the cave, and a fire is lit in the ceiling illuminating a man tide up in the centre.

His body was large, his legs spread out and covered in a dirty fabric. His legs reached Noah's feet as his body is on the ground in silver chains that ran across his body and legs. Only his face was the only thing not covered in chains.

The man breaths heavily and begins to smile at the ground.

"My dear Noah you finally came to see me"

His voice was tempting to the ears. More graceful than the Queen, like a melody that made you transcend to other realms or dimensions. It could put you to sleep if you weren't careful.

"And you bought your friend or should I say your brother now, how lovely of you Noah"

Noah's face is still void of any emotion. He doesn't reply but instead nods his head at him.

"If you could move the hair out of my face so I could get a better look at you that would be much appreciated Noah"

His voice cracks at the end breaking its softness.

Noah steps over his long hair and walks close to his face. He doesn't need to bend over that much as his upper body is huge and built like a warrior.

He touches his hair on his face and moves it behind his ear. His left eye is grey and rotten and only half of his eyeball can actually be seen. It looked to be upside down, up close It turns into a plum colour as he adjusts his eye to look at Noah and Uri. The veins around it are squished together as is the eye. His right eye however is perfectly shaped, a complete contrast to the left.

The strangest thing on him was what was written on his forehead. Uri knew it wasn't in Hebrew but in Arabic as he spent hundreds of years in the middle east. He carefully read it even though Noah warned him not to stare at him for too long. It read's كافر meaning disbeliever which made perfect sense to Uri as he knew who this man was.

He waited half of his life to see the Dajjal. The one called God of the Earth. He will bring wealth to all that follow him as the prophecy goes. Uri and all young vampires heard stories of what he could do, like the ability to change the weather and bring back the dead.

He just hopes he couldn't read peoples thoughts. Rumours are he can't, but some say he doesn't have to; he knows the future and to what it will lead. He was appointed to be here chained for over three thousand years. The man with a body but without a soul that will lead the battle in the end of the world.

Uri quickly looks to the ground as Noah goes back to stand in front of him.

"Now tell me why you two have blessed me with your presence"

Noah knew the Masih knew everything, but he had to play along with his customs.

"We've come from direct orders from the Queen, Masih"

He looks at him in the eye and so does the Dajjal.

"How's your eye, it's been a while since I marked you, hasn't it?"

Noah clenches his jaw. He remembers the day he turned fourteen and was forced to lose his virginity in the temple as the custom is for worshippers of Iblis. He was then sent up to see the Dajjal by a voice that he followed. Everyone searched all night for him, till they realised the Masih's cave was the only place they haven't searched, so the Queen went herself because everyone was so scared to face the beast.

When she got there, she saw Noah lying on the Dajjals lap as the beast traced his nail down his face, specifically on the left like his own scar and ruined Noah's innocence twice in one night. Noah's cries were so sweet to the Dajjal's ears, but the Queen was outraged.

"How dare you touch one of my own" she said to the beast.

"He shall be the future King before I take over" he spoked softly.

He ignores her pleads and digs deeper into Noah's left eye.

"He will be my servant forever; I have marked him"

Noah remembers it every day, constantly having nightmares of him and thus never coming back here no matter if he hears his him call for him or not.

"I found my mate" Noah says with gritted teeth.

"Your mate, well isn't that sweet. What is her name?"

"Laila"

"Her last name?"

Noah stumbles he doesn't know her last name but he's sure Uri might.

"I...I don't know yet Masih"

He smiles and looks towards Uri.

"Maybe your friend knows?"

Uri doesn't respond or show any expression and Noah knows they've fallen for his trap. If he talks to him, he would be serving the Dajjal until he is released. He didn't tell Uri in case any jinn's where over hearing. Noah can't share specific secrets to Uri or anyone that doesn't really belong to the family.

"Laila is all we know for now"

"Why would you lie to me Noah" He asks so softly. Like he's hurt but of course he couldn't be.

"Masih- "

"Are you still scared of your Queen?" He interrupts him. Noah falls silent, he knows the answer to his question, but he doesn't want it to lead down that road.

"Remember Noah, I'm more powerful than her. Once my time comes which is soon, she will be the one in chains" Silence. His words ripping their speech away.

Noah doesn't respond or more like he can't respond because he knows he must be faithful to the future Masih, or he will lose his life even if it that means going against the Queen one day.

"I'm the only one protecting you Noah, if it wasn't for me marking you, you know that Queen of yours would have gotten rid of you and your family"

The Masih glances at Uri.

Noah nods and bows his head in obedience. He knew he was the only one giving him the true power to be King of Jerusalem, without the Masih's mark he would be nothing.

"The queen is preparing you to lead the Jews and Muslims but what you don't know is that when she's finished with you, your dead"

"Dead?"

Noah gapes at him as the Masih smiles and nods.

He doesn't question if he's lying because the Masih's face doesn't show a hint of a lie, or maybe he's been up here so long, he's practised the art of deception.

The Masih al Dajjal starts to stand up his chains rustling from his body. He's double the size of Noah's and more muscular than both of them combined. A small push from him could lead them falling of the mountain. He stood half naked, his hair reaching the ground. Uri could see his leg hairs that were long enough to cover his skin.

"Why would she kill me?"

Masih laughs and smiles at him endearingly.

"Because you'll end up following the religion of Mohammed, like your mate"

Uri looks at Noah surprised that he knew about Laila's faith.

"How- "

"I know what the future holds, King Solomon told me all about you before he trapped me here"

"I won't follow Mohammed that's absurd, I'm faithful to Iblis" Noah says, distort with anger.

"I also had a mate once Noah"

He takes a step closer as far as his chains can take him. The chains burn through his skin leaving another scar on his body, but he doesn't mind. He has several patterns of them across him, some fading and some freshly brewed.

"Her name was Leila, but your mate spells her name with an A instead of an E like mind did"

"I thought you were created without a soul?"

95

"Don't you see Noah, they fed you lies. I had a soul before Allah took it from me"

He walks back so his chains don't burn off his legs and sits back down with his hair covering his face.

"I was once in love you see but I sacrificed her for the greater good"

"Greater good?"

"Yes, if I didn't the prophecy wouldn't come to be, Laila is important to the plan to bring the Jews and Muslims to their death.

"How will she do that?"

Noah's head is spinning but he knew getting a mate would be too good to be true. His entire destiny is to be a slave for the Masih, and he has no idea how he can ever get out of his enslavement.

"I already know your mate more than you will come to know her, for I have given up my soulmate so you could have her instead"

"So, you're saying my mate is really just...yours?"

Noah's voice becomes so quiet.

The Dajjal hums to himself as he stares at the ceiling.

"Laila is neither mine nor yours. She was created from Iblis, and I killed her before Mohammed could come and change her"

"Why would that prophet change her?"

Noah is clearly confused with this information and even Uri begins to lose his composure.

"She follows Mohammed, right?"

"Yes, she follows Mohammed"

Masih nods his head.

"Perfect, and you will too when the day comes"

"I'm not a Muslim and I never will be"

"Noah you must follow Laila, the revolution will come and soon when I come out, I will lead the people and you will be with the army that comes to kill me. Don't ever try to defend me when that day comes"

His tone is deadly serious and his eyes sharp, penetrating into Noah's skull.

Noah can barely respond with this information weighing down on him.

"And when the time comes for me to be free, Uri will be amongst his fellow Jews who fight against me too"

Uri looks up to him, shocked at his words.

"Me?"

Noah looks at Uri his eyes wide because he warned him not to speak.

"Don't worry Noah, I won't make him my slave. Uri is a free man, a believer of God, why do you think I sent him to you?"

Noah closes his eyes and tries to steady his breath.

"What do I do now with all this information"

"Good question my son. First you must get to Laila before the Queen finds her, if you're lucky the Queen still hasn't located her"

"Then?"

"Awaken her"

He knew what he meant but he wants to ask him to make sure.

"You want me to Kill her"

"Yes…before she kills you"

"She couldn't possibly kill me."

"Oh, but she can, she's stronger than the Queen, she is after all my mate"

Noah frowns.

"Keep her blood here with me for me to drink when its time.

"Time?"

"Yes, when it's time for me to get out, I'm going to need my mates blood"

Noah looks at Laila's blood in his hands, he wanted to taste it too. He throws it to him to which he catches it easily.

"You should go now before the sun goes and you have no head start"

"What should I tell the Queen"

Masih huffs and pauses for a while before he speaks.

"From now on you lie, you treat her as your enemy because she does the same to you. And remember don't trust no one, even Laila might betray you after you awaken her"

The Masih steals a glance at Uri again and then back to Noah and smiles.

"Off you go"

The Dajjals cave forms a cage around his body made from stone and slowly kicks out Noah and Uri from inside it. They stare at the rock that once was an open cave and Noah is the first to turn and walk away. His mood relatively low since finding out the only reason he has a mate is because The Masih gave him one.

Noah and Uri make their way down from the mountain both of them not saying a word to each other, digesting what the Dajjal told them.

Uri looks at Noah and coughs to get his attention. Noah shakes off his thoughts and looks over at Uri.

"You, okay?" Uri asks.

"Mmm"

"You know it's okay if you're not I mean heck I wouldn't be after that"

"Man, shut the hell up"

Uri laughs a little and slaps Noah's back.

They walk in silence and before they reach where the temple once was Noah stops in his steps and stares up at the top of the mountain where the Masih resides.

"Come on, you heard him we have to-"

"Shhh"

Noah points to his ear and he points to his left.

A secret tunnel that Dajjal once told Noah about. Noah sniffs the air to make sure no one was around. The Masih's voice is in his head, telling him to go to the tunnel. His voice was faint, but he could hear him. He was used to hearing him

"I know a place"

The Masih told him that the Queens jinn's can't follow him here.

Noah follows the directions the Masih tells him.

"Turn left once you find the lake"

"What?" Uri asks.

"He's in my head"

They reach the lake and there was no left turn.

"What does he mean there's only a right turn"

"Wait for it"

The bushes begin to part ways as does the water in the lake creating a path to the left.

"Wow" Uri gasps.

After they walk out of the path it closes up and they reach the tunnel. It was barricaded with strong vines.

"Help me get them off the door"

Uri lifts off the vines, which try to fight back but they eventually get them off with all their power.

Noah sighs and turns to Uri and reaches for both of his shoulders.

"Uri you know if you come with me, you can never go back to the Kingdom?"

Uri opens his mouth to reply but Noah shakes his head.

"Don't make any jokes. Do you realise what your sacrificing? The Masih is asking us to against the Queen, her army will be after you too. She can't harm me because I'm marked by the Masih but you…she can easily get rid of you"

"It's not like I ever liked the Queen" Uri smiles at him. Noah doesn't smile back and instead pushes him making him stumble back.

"You're not taking this seriously; you'll be sacrificing your life if we get caught"

99

Uri sighs dramatically.

"Yeah, yeah whatever we're wasting time talking, this African blood is gonna expire soon, let's just get to Laila and kill her and we can worry about the Queen later alright?"

Noah sighs and turns around. The tunnel begins to open when he's touches it as the Masih told him to do so in his mind.

Inside the tunnel is scattered in Gold from the floor to the ceiling. The door shuts behind them as they walk inside the Gold maze.

"This will take you to Laila" The Masih instructs.

Chapter Six - Laila dies?

I'm not sure how we've even gotten here. To the point where we're arguing and trying to make sense of our sanity, but I know it needs to end.

"How are you gonna get out of here" Nala asks.

"You mean how are WE gonna get out of here?"

Nala shakes her head, her beautiful afro flying all over her face as she tries to convince me not to leave this place.

"Listen I didn't tell Amen this but for some reason theirs a voice inside me telling me they're going to do something really bad to me"

I look her dead in the eyes as I do up the buttons of my jeans.

"Uri didn't seem that bad?"

"You know I don't trust no one. There's no way I'm gonna wait here for them to find me again I mean even the doctor seemed off?"

"Yeah, I overheard them say he was new, apparently the nurses don't like him"

I put on my leather jacket that I stole from Amen and fix my hijab that was falling of my head.

"Do you know where my pin is?"

"Yeah, it's in my bag"

She goes to search for her bag but can't find it.

"Hey is my bag next to you?"

I look over in my area and theirs nothing, but tissues scattered around that I didn't notice before. Their covered in small specks of blood and the smell is too strong for me making me dizzy.

"Did you find my bag?"

Nala comes over to look at what I'm staring at.

"Oh, Amen accidently scratched himself too hard, you know how he gets when he's on edge"

I remember being in the hospital before mum was pronounced dead amen picked on his finger until blood came out. I didn't stop him, because I was too numb to react to anything but that was the only time, I saw him like that.

"I'm sorry I scared you guys"

I turn to Nala and hug her.

"I didn't feel anything though"

She looks at my neck and gives me a questioning look.

"You didn't notice the marks on your neck? You know before they weirdly cleared up"

I shake my head. I can feel them on me, it's just a feeling that there's something heavy on my left side of my neck but I couldn't feel any pain.

"It wasn't painful when he bit me, I felt safe"

It was weird saying that aloud, but I know Nala wouldn't judge me. We had weirder conversations. A year ago, she would listen to me talk about how much I enjoyed the feeling of a pin going through my skin and she wouldn't react, strangely or judge me. I knew deep down though she thinks I'm crazy, but she listened to me anyway until those desires left me.

"Oh, theirs my bag"

It was under the hospital bed. She fiddles through it and hands me a pin. I Place it in my hijab and make sure Its secured.

"Do you have gloss? My lips are so cracked"

"Yeah, I do, you look like a crackhead babe"

She hands me it and I put it on generously, hiding my sickly face.

"Well, this crackhead is getting out of here, come on"
Nala looks at me, her face screaming at me not to go so I
take her hand and drag her out. I open the door only an inch
to see who's outside.

"Are they out there?" Nala whispers behind my back.

"There's one nurse behind the desk, we have to crouch
down, follow me"
The nurse is distracted on the phone, so I crouch down and
open the door just enough to move our bodies outside. Nala
crouches down too and we walk out our knees cracking
with every step. As soon as we get to the desk, trying our
best not to make any noise we hear Amens loud voice
coming from the hallway that leads to our floor.

"Toilet" Nala mouths to me.
She pushes me to the toilet at the end of the hallway. I
watch the nurse spin on her chair and as soon as she faces
the other side, we make a quiet run for it, with our backs
still bent.
When we reach the toilet, I turn around to see if anyone
spotted us and we both see Amens figure emerging at the
end of the hallway talking to two other police officers.

"Hurry" Nala pushes me inside.

"Arrghhh, it stinks like shit in here" I state the obvious.
Nala puts her hands over my mouth.

"Their gonna go inside and see were not there we have to
just go back" Nala whispers.

"Nala, Amen won't let me leave until I tell him how I got
two holes in bloody neck and how it healed so quickly.
They won't believe me if I start talking about demons and
shit. You know they'll send me straight to a whack house"

"Lower your voice"
Amen and the officers where chattering outside. They still
haven't gone in yet.

"I'll be on some kind of suicide watch and not to
mention those guys will end up finding me"

"Do you think their after you cause of what you saw"

I nod my head.

"I don't think I was meant to see it"

"But if you were able to then maybe"

Amens voice cuts her off.

"I'm gonna check up on them in abit, I think they both need some space" Amen says.

He's so close to us and we're still both in this stinking toilet.

"Shit" we both say

"What we gonna do now"

Nala puts her hands under neath her chin and closes her eyes. Something she does before coming up with a genius plan. I look at her, knowing full well she's going to take my side and find a way to get out of here.

She looks up at me with serious bright eyes.

"As soon as they realise, you're not in there I'll get out and pretend a nurse took you to the toilet. Once you hear them leaving, I'll meet you at the back stairs. That will take us to the back parking lot and then five minutes away is"

"Grenwell park" I interrupt.

"Yes, I'll tell Jay to meet us there in five"

"Fuck, I love you"

I hug her but she quickly gets out of my hug.

"I can hear them reaching the door. Bye" she says quickly.

She reaches for the door and pretends to act surprised when she sees them. I can slightly hear them talk. I put my ears behind the door trying to concentrate on her words.

An unnatural gust of wind rushes into the bathroom ripping through my clothes. I'm too scared to turn around because I can feel a strong animal like presence behind me.

Somebody coughs behind me alerting me that I'm not alone and I freeze my heart beating out of my chest.

"Who you listening to?" A familiar voice says.

I turn around slowly to see Uri.

"You"

He smiles. Mischief is all I can describe this man as he looks at me like he won a prize.

"So, you're here? I had a hunch you still didn't escape"

What kind of psycho is he?

My hands are trembling, and his smile grows even more when he realises. He takes a step towards me.

"Wait please, I didn't do anything to you. Why are you back for me?"

I have a feeling I know the answer to that. He doesn't respond and instead keeps getting closer to me.

I turn around to leave.

"They all think you tried to kill yourself"

I stop reaching for the door and turn around to him.

"What?"

"Even your brother thinks so"

His smile has completely washed away.

"If you go to them now, they'll take you away from him"

He puts his hands in his pockets

"No, they think I just fainted"

I shake my head.

"Oh, they just said that to not put on edge. Think about it Laila. You were all alone upstairs, who else could have done that to you. I overheard Amen and the Doctor mention you had a past history of this kind of behaviour? They said maybe seeing Nala like that triggered you. Is that true?" he asks me, mockingly.

I look down at my hands filled with past scars and my hidden legs that are filled with stories, I'd rather keep to myself. I couldn't answer him because in this moment I felt weak and helpless.

"St...Stop" I try to say.

He walks closer to me his body now so close to mine, I can almost hear his heartbeat as our breaths mingle in the small space, he created between us.

"If you come with me, I'll keep you safe"

I shake my head. I can feel the tears forming around my eyes.

"I know I shouldn't have seen that ceremony"

"Don't talk about that here"

He looks around him, which I find odd. There's no one else in here but him and me.

"Noah is waiting for you in your room"

"Noah?"

"Yes, he was the one that bit you. You appeared to him in Aaliyah's body remember? Anyway, he wants to see you"

"I remember him in the room with you as well"

His eyebrows knit together.

"What room?" he says lightly.

I cross my arms around my body. I'm not sure if I should let him know about the room since he doesn't want me to speak about anything here.

"The room...with heads?"

His mouth hangs open.

"How did you see us?" he asks angrily.

He grabs my neck aggressively.

"Are you some kind of Sorceress? How did you see us?"

I gasp in the shock of his tight grip around my neck. His hand blocking any air circulation.

"You literally came to me just now and gave me your bracelet so I can stop seeing things"

"That wasn't me"

"N...No it was" I kick him, but he doesn't budge.

Nala and Amens voice are overheard.

"WHERE IS SHE?" Amens voice yells.

"I swear a nurse took her to the toilet" Nala says.

"We need to go" he says.

He lets go of my neck and I almost collapse gasping for air. He drags me to the wall opposite us and puts his hands inside the wall.

"What are you doing?"

"Getting us out of here" he says without looking at me. His hand going inside the wall.

"How are you doing that?"

"Yeah, yeah I get it you've never seen someone walk through a wall but now's not the time to act surprised. We need to leave so grab my hand and close your eyes"
I take a deep breath and grab his hand.
He moves his body steadily inside the wall, making a cracking noise as if his body is breaking through it. Though there's no sign of any crack in the wall, it looks painful.
The bathroom door opens, and I turn to see Amen. We stare at each other perplexed, his body in a fighting stance and his eyes confused and frantic. His mouth hung wide open looking between me and Uri who's fully inside the wall and all he can do is watch as I'm pulled inside the wall and his face is gone from my vision.
I close my eyes like Uri told me to and feel my body feeling light as a feather, Like I weighed nothing.
I didn't stop to think how it would feel like to be inside a wall because everything was happening so quickly my brain can't even process it right, but it's the most adrenaline I've felt in a long time.
I can still feel Uri's grip on my hand it feels tightly secured to m.
There's a lot of heavy sounds I can hear around me that sounded like the wind was talking. It was like I was moving but my feet weren't on the ground. It was just a bunch of mushy air surrounding me.
My head is pulling me to the other side, and I'm slowly dragged out the other end. I can finally feel my body weight and it feels heavier that I nearly have to hold onto Uri for balance.
 My feet are on the ground, and it feels stimulating to have them be connected to a surface area. The carpet looks like the one in my room, a brown Persian rug Amen bought me for my birthday last month. I look at my hand that's still

holding his and when we lock eye's he lets go off me quickly. I realise we are in fact in my room as Uri said, but it was much cleaner than I left it last night.

"Hope you don't mind I cleaned up whilst I waited for you"
A man's voice startles me, it was familiar with the same deep huskiness as I remember.
He comes out of the corner of my room, a dark shadow hiding him, but I can see his scar dragging down from his eye and it makes me nervous like it did before. His jet-black hair falls on his forehead as he just holds on to my eyes.
I couldn't say anything back to him, I felt too shy to speak to someone so, so, ethereal? It was as if he was hard to read like he has barrier around him, but he drew me in, nevertheless. His eyes feel perilous, and I want them to keep staring at me more but Uri coughs, breaking our eye contact.

"I'll make sure no one comes in" he says to Noah.

"Thanks"
My mind comes back to reality, and I start panicking again.

"You realise Amen will come straight here, right? He knows I'd want to see my dad before running away"
Uri smirks to Noah and leaves my room, shutting the door, completely ignoring me. I feel too humiliated to look at Noah. The silence feeling uncomfortable, and it's just dawned on me that he's with me in my room…alone. The same man that tasted my blood.
Noah walks back into the shadow the sun slowly reaching his face. The small glimpse I got of the rest of him makes me want to see more and without realising I take a step forward.

"Close the curtains please" he asks agitated by the sun. The sun rise was coming to an end and my black curtains were wide open, the way I left them last night.

I walk over to them, doing exactly what he asked for and I slowly close them.

I can hear his footsteps, so I look over my shoulder to see him in the centre of my room staring at my drawings. Some drawings I did when I was nearly passed out. Amen always hated them because he said they were haram and go against Islam.

"You look abit too religious to draw these?"

There was a hint of a tease in his tone. I should respond, being silent will just make me look more of a freak.

"I can't draw now because I'm a Muslim?"

"Your right"

I said that so quietly, I'm surprised he heard.

He puts his hands across my art and drags his hand down to one of my most demonic drawings and rips it out of the wall.

"HEY"

I walk over to him, his back towards me. How dare he just rip it out like that.

He doesn't turn around or flinch by my sudden tone.

"These symbols, you know what they can do?"

He turns around and shows me my drawing of Satan dressed in a Hinata cosplay.

"I drew that when I was 12" I shrug.

"These can attract creatures to you Laila. Creatures that can fall in love with you and slowly eat your soul away"

He takes a step closer to me, his eyes piercing through mine. He looks angry like I did something wronged him but all I think about is the way he just said my name. It feels like it belongs to him. It rolled out his tongue so perfectly like he was the one that named me.

"Once they attach themselves to you, it will be very hard to get rid of them"

His tone was so low that I couldn't make out that I had to watch his mouth move to make out what he was saying but his lips were so plump and wet that I didn't care what came out of them.

"Laila?"

"They're just symbols"

I snatch the drawing out of his hand and stick it back on the wall, trying to get a grip of my emotions.

"Satan is just another living being like us, maybe he just shows us our true nature. You know the one hidden deep inside us"

I don't turn around; his eyes are too intense on my back that I almost feel threatened by him. It's as if he wants to harm me but I don't want to start panicking again. A strong pit in my stomach was telling me to run but all I was doing was standing still waiting for him to tell me why he was looking for me.

"Satan can destroy your life or fix it, that's all dependent if your faithful to him"

He comes close behind me. His footsteps are light and cautious, like he was scared of me.

"Faithful?"

"Being his servant in every way. Anything he asks of you; you do without hesitation"

"I guess were all slaves to Him"

"How so?"

He takes another step behind me, his shadow reflecting on my wall.

"He controls the System we live in, doesn't he?"

My breathing is steady, like I know exactly what I'm talking about but deep down I don't think I do. My mouth and thoughts feel disconnected. I'm not sure if I have full control of what I'm saying.

"He does"

I can feel his breath caressing the back of my neck.

He's a step away from touching me, and I know right now all I want is for him to take one more step so I can finally feel him again.

110

"Then everyone living in his system is his slave"
He doesn't respond but just breaths heavily on the back of my neck, so I keep going.

"Until we escape everything he has created is when we can have true free will. Even those that are faithful to him, their no different to us"

"Us?"

He moves towards me again and our bodies touch ever so subtlety, like a feather faintly skimming through you, but I feel an inhuman sensation drift through my body. It snuggled inside like it finally found it's home. I didn't know what to make of it, I just closed my eyes wondering what this foreign feeling is.

"Us" I breath.

He leans into my ear.

"You know I'm not a human Laila" he whispers.

I open my eyes and turn around to him breaking through my thoughts and see someone that doesn't look like Noah. His eyes were completely pitch black and his face was dishevelled with his skin turning pale. He resembled my drawing of Satan, but he still had his normal features like his scar and his facial features. His veins however stuck out of his face and his hair was standing up defying gravity. His nose kept moving into different shapes as did his mouth which was closed. Something was growing in his face and all I could do was stare helplessly at this creature.

"I know you're not human" I whisper.

I'm witnessing his true form and yet I'm standing still as a worthless statue. Something was slowly growing inside his mouth. His lips were growing bigger as a sharp object stuck through.

Teeth as sharp as knifes, extends out to his chin. They were shiny and I caught my reflection on them. The same ones that dug deep inside my neck that created clarity in my mind.

111

He watches me breathless as he transforms and settles into this body that was ugly to the human eye but to me it was unadulteratedly pure.

His saliva dripping down on my cheek as I let it, he can't close his mouth because his teeth were too big. His saliva was warm unlike his body that I could feel pressed on to me now.

"Would you like to be like me Laila?"

His tone was noticeably clear, the clearest he's been. I smile at him knowing I could never truly be like him.

"I can never be like you"

My face was leaning towards his, moving on its own. I wanted to touch his fangs. They sparkle in my eyes. It was like I was aware how dangerous he was, but I didn't let fear control me anymore. A stronger desire took place and vanquished the fearful irritable sound of reason.

"If you give me your heart, you can be just like me, I just need your permission"

He looks at me with so much lust dripping out of his eyes and skin that I almost nod my head. I don't know if he wanted to eat me seeing me as a meal or he actually sees me the same way I was seeing him.

"Why does it cost my heart?"

I almost don't recognise my voice. I know my heart means the end of my life but nonetheless to be powerful like them would make me fear nothing. I would no longer feel helpless, but would such a sacrifice be worth my heart?

"Because you'll no longer need it Laila"

"But what if I want it back?"

He smiles at me slyly and twists his neck to the right and looks down at me endearingly.

"You won't want it back, once you feel the power consume you, you'd never even think of going back to being human"

It all seems too good to be true as I shake my head at the idea of that kind of power. It would feel like I'm doing a deal with the devil.

"Does it hurt? Would I go to Hell?"

He reaches for my heart and digs his nails on the surface, breaking through my clothes and skin without difficulty.

"Only for a little while"

He ignores the question of Hell, but he glowers at me waiting for my answer. His nails not moving from my skin, and I know he can feel that I've lost control of my body, one small move and he can eat me alive. His chest puffed out as he snarls at me waiting for my answer.

"I-"

Unfortunately, I can't finish what I want to say because Uri come's crashing through the door.

"They're coming"

Noah shuts his eyes and looks back at me with so much agitation. He shakes his face shifting back to his normal handsome self.

"What's your answer Laila?"

I know my answer will be no because I couldn't give up my humanity as that would mean my place in Heaven. Before Mama died, she told me a secret and said only I can know. She said if the Shaytan ever asks for your soul know you will never get it back without a sacrifice, I thought it was one of her midnight talks but I remember she made me look her in her eyes and promise that I will never do such a thing. She thought I was a demon child. I sometimes would overhear her on the phone to her sister talking about me and how I would talk to other demons, that I was apparently 'already communicating with them'.

She was always hesitant around me like I was made up of evil. Constantly dragging me to a mosque to get rid of 'Shaytan who was inside of me' as the sheikhs would say. So, I shake my head in order to not disappoint her if she was looking down at me.

"I'm sorry I can't"

Both of them look at me in surprise.

"What"

Noah clenches his jaw like he wasn't expecting that answer.

I wanted to see him again, for a reason that wasn't pure or reasonable. So instead, I just pleaded with my eyes for him to stay or take me with him even if he didn't take my heart.

"Noah, we don't have time"

Uri locks the door and bares his fangs at me. I can hear Amens voice and serval others barging through the front door. Police sirens where railing through the streets making all of our heads hurt.

Noah looks at me one more time his eyes desperate for me to say yes but I can't disappoint my mum. Years of her trying to fix me going down the drain would just kill me. It's the least I could do for her. She'd always look at me in pain for talking to those spirits in my room and now I understood why.

"Noah, you have to do it NOW"

He shakes his head.

"I can't"

"If you don't than betraying the Queen was in vein"

"The Queen?" I ask.

I have no idea what their talking about, but several police officers were outside the room already.

"LAILA" Amen shouts outside the door.

He tries to open it, but Uri's body was holding it closed.

"Laila, I tracked your phone I know you're in there, open the door. I believe you now Laila just please open the God damn door"

"You want to be King; you want the power of the Masih?"

Noah nods his head.

"THAN KILL HER"

I knew Amen heard that, but I hoped he didn't.

114

"WHO'S IN THERE, DON'T TOUCH HER" Amen
shouts.
He tries to knock down the door.
   "Why do you want to kill me"
Uri looks at me in disgust and Noah just looks at me as if
he's void of any emotion.
   "Get rid of your damn feelings she isn't your real mate
remember, she's the Masih's"
Noah pushes Uri out of the way and stares at me with a
blank expression like the one I saw through the mirror.
Something clicked in his mind and the way he looked at me
before completely washed away with Uri's words. He
captured the look of a villain that had no guilt.
   "I'm sorry Laila"
Just like that in one swift movement his hand is inside my
body and around my heart. My bones crushing feels too
painful that I scream out loud. One second my heart was
inside me and then it was outside my body in his hand. His
hand filled with my blood, and I look down at my chest an
empty hole as my bones scatter around my feet. I was so
numb.
   "Why can't I feel it?"
   "Because you're a demon, my dear Laila"
Amen knocks down my door with four police officers
behind him. Uri and Noah run off through the wall behind
me.
   "Laila?"
Amen and the police look at me with shock and I turn
around to Noah his face not fully through the wall yet.
My heart in his hand as he looks at me standing frozen
watching him with tears in my eyes touching my empty
chest.
Noah licks my heart and then puts it in his mouth and
swallows it whole.
The police all drop their guns shocked at the sight, as was I.
I couldn't move my body afraid if I did move, I would feel

the pain of my heart missing even more. But when Noah escapes through the wall and I'm left alone with Amen and the officers I slowly collapse to the floor.

Amen runs towards me and holds my body before it hits the floor and I smile at him. He's the best brother I could ever ask for.

"I'm sorry" he says crying uncontrollably.

"Where's Nala?" I ask him before I close my eyes, feeling my body deteriorate into pieces of stone. I have no connection to my body anymore, everything I used to feel just vanished in seconds. I was just a pair of eyes watching myself become lifeless in Amen's arms.

]

Chapter Seven ~ The heart of your mate.

In Jerusalem, a protest started in the morning after several weeks of new cases of missing boys have gone ignored. The first incident was a Jewish boy who went missing for three days until his body was found floating in a pool with his neck barely hanging to his head. The next case followed a Muslim boy who was missing for a week until yesterday evening his body was discovered on the shore of the beach with his head tied to his stomach.

The Israeli and Palestinian government still silent about the murders causing a surge of anger through the public.

The protest started off peacefully in the morning but now as the day begins to darken people from both groups have decided to riot, both blaming the 'other' of the crimes.

The extremist groups on both parties have come out to the streets of Jerusalem with weapons even the police don't carry, causing utter chaos.

Women are crying from injuries as cars are ramming onto the buildings and pedestrians. Young guys were setting fires to buildings and some engaging in full on ambushed gang fights. Even restaurants and workplaces have been broken into, leading to the news labelling this the most criminal day in Jerusalem.

Meanwhile as crowds of people run off to safety, Noah and Uri walk slowly on the streets unfazed by the rioting. Noah walks ahead of Uri who watches him with his hands in his pockets. Noah stares aimlessly at the people.

"Idiots"

Uri doesn't say anything his mind still on Laila. He didn't think Noah would have the guts but when he saw her heart taken out, he felt miserable for a reason he couldn't explain. He didn't want to say anything because he shouldn't feel this way, his main goal was to help Noah become the King of Jerusalem.

"How many people do you think the Queen wants dead today?" Noah asks.

Uri shrugs, he knows Noah can't see him, but he isn't in the mood to speak.

Noah doesn't want to look at Uri, he's been silent ever since they left Laila and Noah knew the first thing, he'd ask would be about why he hesitated. He knew why he hesitated, but Uri would just remind him why he shouldn't have. He knew if he wanted to be King and safe from the Queen, he has to listen to the Masih.

A Palestinian boy throws a rock towards Uri and Noah blocks it from hitting Uri. Uri didn't even notice.

"Uri? That could have hit you"

Uri doesn't respond and instead just walks off in front of Noah. He thinks about what Laila said about the bracelet and how she saw him in the man's room. The blood that made him frantic was hers. He also knew it wasn't him who gave her the bracelet so was this why they got the blood sample so easily, he thought. It was practically handed to them by the doctor. They were in a hurry to get to the temple that they didn't ask any questions but maybe they should have.

Noah sighs and walks beside him. He knows he should start the conversation, but Uri was a pain in the ass sometimes.

"Go on, just ask me. Why did I hesitate right that's what's got you so mute"?

Uri looks away from him. Watching the old man get beat up by some young kids.

"No actually I want to know why you ate her heart?"
Noah stops walking clearly not expecting that question. Uri doesn't stop and instead walks ahead of him and shouts to the sky.

"WHY EAT HER HEART?"

"Bro lower your voice"
Uri takes of his Kippa smothers it in Noah's face, behaving like a crazy man.
Noah grabs him by the collar and shakes him. Uri is still unfazed, no one notices them too preoccupied on rioting.

"They're watching us"
Uri swats Noah's hands away from his shirt and he fix's his collar. They both start walking again as the riots attract the army's attention.

"We need to hide before the Queen finds us"

"I can see why the Masih chose you"

"Yeah, why's that?"
Uri pauses for a second thinking carefully before he says something he regrets.

"I won't take offense"
They walk towards an apartment building, that's under construction.

"Well, I didn't think you'd do it...you know take her heart"

"Or eat it?"

On the inside Noah was dying from guilt but on the outside Uri thought he enjoyed eating her heart. Noah remembers her face when she saw her heart taken out. She was helpless. If only she said yes, then he wouldn't feel trapped in this cycle of guilt.

He had to look unfazed in front of Uri because he knew Uri needed him to be strong if they're going to escape the Queen's questions. Uri could act like he didn't care but Noah knew he was nervous for what the future holds.

"Why did you eat it?" Uri asks again but this time making sure no one could hear.

Noah opens the door of the apartment building, and they walk towards the elevator. It was a rundown building that the Palestinians lived in, who were mostly poor. The walls we're damp and the wallpapers we're barely hanging onto the walls. Noah pressed the button to the elevator, and they waited for it to arrive, looking behind them every few seconds to check if no one was coming.

"If I didn't then the Queen will eventually end up taking it if she found out, even if we buried it somewhere she'd still find it, you know how skilled her dogs are"

"Or we could have given it to the Masih?"

"He would have told me if he wanted it. But I think he didn't because the Queen probably put eyes on him since we didn't return to her immediately"

Uri nods his head and walks up and down the hallway.

"But still, you think the Masih would want you to eat his mates heart?"

Noah clenches his jaw and looks at him heatedly.

The elevator door opens and a Muslim girl with a pink hijab and a pastel purple dress stood inside waiting. She didn't leave and instead they all just watched each other.

"Are you going up?" Noah asks.

The girl shakes her head and points down with her finger. She was carrying books in her hand and a unicorn pencil case on top of her books.

Noah peers at Uri.

"You can go ahead" Uri says.

He had a big fake smile on his face. The girl didn't smile back and proceeded to press the -11 button to take her down.

When it closed Noah turned around.

"What are you doing? We should of went down with her"

"How did it taste?"

Uri leans back on a wall opposite Noah.

"Tasted like a heart" Noah sighs.

"Mmm yes I know what a fucking heart tastes like but how did HER heart taste like. He told us she was born from Iblis. You know what that means?"

"YES, I KNOW"

Noah grabs his hair in annoyance.

"If you know then why would you risk it, she's not even your bloody mate"

Noah opens his eyes.

"Don't say that"

Uri comes off the wall and strides over to Noah.

"What? That she's not your-"

Noah grabs him and pushes him on the elevator door. Uri was expecting him to react this way, hence why he looks at him with pity.

"SHE IS MY MATE"

Uri laughs so loud that the even the walls begin to shake.

"Wow, don't you see Noah, don't you see how he's fooled you"

Noah looks into his eyes and realises Uri is trying to see if he spins out of control then he will just prove Uri right. Noah has been feeling sick ever since he ate her heart. He wanted to taste her blood again even a taste of her organs. He knew he felt jealous of the Masih having her blood.

"I ate it so she can never go back to being human, that's all end of conversation" Noah lies.

He breaths heavily and lets go of Uri as the elevator door opens again, this time empty.

Uri stumbles into it and Noah walks in and presses -11 and the doors shut. As the elevator goes down a violin floats on top of them playing classical music. They look at each other, both silently having a conversation with their eyes. They know the violin is a spy for the Queen and once they step into the station underground, they'll be summoned with an army of supernatural's.

121

"-5"

Uri says looking up at the violin. Noah's fists we're clenched. He knew he couldn't go back up. He would just have to be convincing. If he ran away from the Queens army the situation would get severely worse.

"Well London was quiet the trip"

Noah raises his eyebrow and Uri winks as if to say just go with it.

"Yeah, quiet the trip" Noah replies.

Floor -7 was approaching, and Noah was beginning to sweat with nerves.

"It's a shame you ate her, we could have bought a peace of her to The Queen"

Noah sighs, this wouldn't convince the Queen and if it did, he would be more worried.

"The Queen wouldn't care as long as she's dealt with" Noah goes along with Uri's game.

"Yeah, well be prepared to get an earful"

Noah looks at Uri his eyes wide open.

"Stuff like that will get you killed"

"I'm already dead so why not"

Uri's smile is up to his eye's, and they wrinkle into the corner of them, naturally Noah can't help but smile back.

"Yeah, being actually dead would be nice for a change"

The elevator stopped at -10 and the boys become serious. It's doors opens and the same Muslim girl from first floor appears however this time her purple dress is deep maroon colour, and she has on a black hijab. The only thing she carries is a machete knife dripping in blood in her right hand. Around her was a pile of dead bodies, some still sputtering out blood.

– 10 was another station floor where people would go from one dimension to another instead of inner Earth which was -11. The elevator is about to close but she puts her knife in between the door.

"Hurry before they wake up"

Noah and Uri step out, the violin disappearing as they do so.

"Who are you?" Noah asks.

She pushes her knife in her dress, the dress sucks the knife hiding it.

"I've been sent by the Masih"

She walks across the dead the bodies, stepping on some of them and they both follow behind her. Her face is completely blank like she's killed these many supernatural's before.

"How do we know you're telling the truth"

"He knows you ate her heart. But that's not why he sent me"

The station lights flickered as they waited for the train to arrive. The people on the floor were mostly vampires and they would come back alive in a few minutes if they didn't hurry.

"If you went to the last floor, the Anesh were waiting for you. They were going to ambush you"

"Damn I knew she was listening to us"

Noah's fangs extend in frustration. Uri stares at the girl, he was impressed she could kill at least a hundred vampires in the station. It was a dark station that had old red wine chairs for people to wait till their next train and a velvet brown carpet on the floor that was filled with bodies. There were two platforms, one on the left and one on the right. The train approaches and It was empty, only the driver who was a ghost was controlling the train, but he wasn't even paying attention to the bodies on the floor, his eyes on a puzzle in front of him.

They walk in, Noah and Uri sit opposite to her. The doors still don't close and one of the vampires who was a man wearing a suit wakes up. He clicks his neck and looks around flustered at the mess. The girl looks at him and he goes back to closing his eyes, playing dead as his body trembles in fear.

The door finally closes, and the train begins to move. It was too fast for any human to go on, but they could withstand it.

"Are you gonna tell us your name at least"
Uri asks and puts his hands on his knees observing the girl.

"I don't have a name…anymore"

"What was your name before?"
She opens her hand, and a black flame comes out of it, and it spells her name in Arabic.

"Amina"

"How old are you?"

"I'm 14"
Noah and Uri share a look. She looked young but how was a 14-year-old able to kill so many vampires on her own.

"I'm trained by the Masih since I escaped the Kingdom when I was 6"
She looks at Noah who shakes his head. They both know the Queen steals kids and babies for the Kingdom to feast on and change into vampire slaves but for one to escape was unheard of.

"So, the Masih knew this would happen, he knew the Queen would follow us?"
The girl smirks.

"She already knows about the Masih's mate"

"Look we knew this would happen but why would the Queen even send us to Him if she knows Laila is his mate"
The train stops and she gets up. She touches her dress as she waits for her machete to come out.
Noah and Uri follow her out of the station doors. They stepped out to forest covered in black smoke. The black smoke in these woods were shadow people, who didn't belong to the Kingdom as they were hard to capture and manipulate. The shadow people lived isolated and barely anyone would ever want to hang around them.

"He told me to escort you here until Laila wakes from the dead"

"Yeah, that's nice but you didn't answer my question"

"Uri" Noah hisses.

"What she's stalling and it's pissing me off"

The girl walks ahead her knife tightly secured in her right hand. She waves of the shadows with her knife, making a pathway.

"It's so dark"

Uri is clearly annoyed.

"And it fucking stinks"

Noah nods, shadow people weren't the cleanest but that's how they kept people away from them.

"I can't light a fire; we'd attract too much attention to us"

The trees were howling at the unwanted guests and the shadows were angrily running around them trying to kick them out.

"How far are we going?"

"We're nearly there"

Vines from trees we're attacking their legs, but they were too quick for the vines. Amina's reaction time reminded Noah of Aaliyah, moving without hesitation. Her reflex was alien for someone her age.

She stops outside a cabin. It looked destroyed and abandoned.

"When I open the door, run in before any shadow people follow us inside"

They both nod and look behind them, a swarm of shadow people were running towards them. Their bodies barely touching the ground as they flew in the air at a dangerous speed.

"Well, you better hurry and open that door" Uri says.

She puts her hands out and a black flame comes out and opens the lock on the door. Uri opens it instead and ends up burning himself as he stumbles inside. Noah pushes himself inside and Amina fights of the shadow people.

"HURRY!" Noah shouts.

Amina throws herself inside and shuts the door with her flame.

"Shit Uri"

Noah looks at Uris burnt hand.

"Didn't I tell you not to touch the door?" Amina says.

Uri hisses in pain.

"No, you didn't"

Noah looks at the inside of the cabin forgetting Uris tantrum. It was cozy. He always wanted to live somewhere with a fireplace and bookshelves. It smelt like cinnamon and fresh laundry. The walls inside where painted brown and there were posters of Elvis and the Beatles. A record player near a sofa caught his attention. He walks over to it and touches it. It had piles of dust on it, but he didn't mind. Uri drops on the sofa and puts one of his leg up on the wooden table and sighs.

"I'm fucking exhausted mate"

Uri closes his eyes. Noah looks at Amina who is putting a spell on the door.

She whispers it under her breath, her mouth barely moving as a purple bubble surrounds the door. Noah stands beside Uri as she finishes the spell.

"Thank you for saving us"

"Saving us? Who knows she could be working for the Queen, hell we could be in her trap right now"

Amina rolls her eyes.

"You can sit down you know?"

She points to the sofa to Noah.

"Yeah, I'm not really in the sitting mood"

He walks around the cabin and wonders what the Masih has in store for him. It seems even Amina is a slave to the beast just like he is and although it's nice not to be alone, his mind thinks of how many slaves could the Masih have and could his be bigger than the Queen's army.

Amina walks over to the kitchen and flicks the kettle on. Theirs already water in it making Noah and Uri both question if anyone was in here before.

"You've been here before?" Uri asks.

Amina shakes her head.

"It's my mother's"

Uri puts his legs down and sits up straight.

"I thought you were a slave; how do you know your mum?"

Amina pours herself a tea.

"You want some tea?"

Noah sighs.

"Seriously just answer the question we're tired"

Amina sits down opposite Uri next to the fireplace on a rocking chair.

"Masih promised me I can see my mother if I bring you to safety"

"And if you didn't?"

Noah asks sitting down next to Uri.

She looks at her tea avoiding their eyes.

"He said that she'd die because of my incompetence"

She takes a swing at her tea. Uri and Noah peek at each other, raising their brows.

"How do you know she even exists?"

"Uri!"

"What? the Masih can deceive anyone, especially a 14 year-old"

Noah closes his eyes and rests his head back.

"I know, he could have lied but it was worth a shot, I have nothing more to lose. I already lost my faith"

"Your faith? Your still wearing a headscarf, you don't look like you have"

"I only wore it today in case I see her, but the Masih doesn't like his slaves wearing one"

"Your mum, is she a Muslim?" Uri asks.

127

"Yes"

"And your dad?"

"He was a Jew. He was a spy who married my mum"

"What happened to him?"

Noah sits up and asks her sincerely.

"I killed him"

There was an awkward silence in the air. Even Uri couldn't come up with something funny to say to break to the tension.

"Yeah, sometimes I think of killing my dad too"

"Uri that's not funny"

"I wasn't trying to be"

"You don't even have a dad"

Uri nodded in agreement he didn't have one, but he thought if he did, he'd sure want to kill him for throwing him away to the streets.

Amina throws the rest of her tea in the fire and the glass. The fire begins to eat up her mug.

"My dad was a slave to the Queen; he was captured for being a wizard. He had to spy on my mum because she was part of the Muslim rebellion underground. She was a witch too, the most powerful one, she had led the Palestinian witches in the rebellion but when my father fell in love with her the Queen captured me and years later made me kill him"

"If your parents were witches, how did the Queen make you kill him"

"I was 6, my powers came in a few months later she timed it well"

"Right" Noah nods.

"That's when the Masih saved me, I followed his voice outside the temple and found him. He promised to save my mother, but I had to devout myself to him and not the Queen"

"How did you escape the Queen's spell"

Amina smiles.

"The Dajjal isn't just deceptive, his power doesn't even compare to the Queens, once you touch him you no longer fear her, you only fear him"

Amina looks at her hands which begin to emerge with a tattoo, with foreign writing.

"I have the same one"

Noah pulls up his sleeves and extends his arm, the same tattoo begins to emerge and stops at his elbow.

"It's the mark of the Beast, it's a map"

"A map to what" Uri asks.

Amina shrugs. Noah was hoping she would know.

"I still can't figure it out. This language isn't in any book in the world. Trust me I've searched" Noah says.

"Anyone that touches the beast gets the same mark"

Amina looks at them.

"Do you know how many he's touched?" Noah asks.

A gust of wind comes in through the window.

"My guess is a few have this mark, but the Queen still holds her power"

One window begins to shake rapidly. It was above the kitchen sink and the wind was damaging it.

"What's happening?"

They all get up.

"Laila's happening"

Noah and Uri look at her confused.

"She's waking up"

Noah begins to feel sick as Amina tries to seal the window with a spell.

"Where's the toilet" Noah asks.

He begins to feel something crawl up his stomach like it wants to come out immediately.

Amina points to the corner of the room right beside the kitchen. He rushes inside and leaves the door open as he throws up in the sink. His entire body shaking profusely. Uri looks at Noah collapse on the bathroom floor, but he doesn't help him up. He just stares at the heart in the sink as Noah slowly passes out into a deep sleep.

"Fuck"

Amina finishes her spell and walks into the bathroom.

"Is that her heart?"

"Yeah"

Uri kneels down to Noah and slaps his cheeks. He doesn't respond.

"He's out"

Uri carries him out the bathroom.

"He shouldn't have eaten it"

"Well, we didn't exactly have a guidebook to killing the Masih's mate, did we?"

He drops Noah on the sofa.

"What now? What happens when she wakes up?"

Amina looks at Uri her eyes wide awake.

"She's going to want her heart back"

Amina brings out her sword from her leg and sits on the rocking chair, making it face the door of the cabin.

"What's got you so scared? Laila isn't going to kill you, she's harmless"

Amina plays with her knife, restlessly.

"She's not human. You've awakened her now. She can kill anyone in sight. Someone born from Iblis doesn't like their things taken away from them"

Uri shakes his head laughing at the idea of Laila killing anyone. The last time he saw her she was intimidated by him.

"Even if she was a demon, she believes Noah's her mate she couldn't harm us"

Amina doesn't look at him and continues to look at the Cabin door.

"Didn't the Masih tell you?"

"Tell us what"

Uri stands in front of her, blocking her view of the door. She looks up at him, her eyes still wide with fear.

"When she dies, she will no longer care about her mate"
Uri looks at her with his arms crossed still not
understanding what she means.

"The reason why the Dajjal killed her was because she
wanted to kill him"
Noah uncrossed his hands and looks at Noah, realisation
hitting him like a brick.

"She'll be after Noah, not the Masih" Uri says to himself
as he stares at Noah.

"Yeah, and I have to protect him from Laila and the
Queen so he can be king, and I can finally see my mum"

"But why did he want to awaken her?"
Amina stands up her sword in her right hand ready to use.

"Because he needs his mate to break free from his prison
that Solomon put him in. Prophet Solomon controlled the
jinn's before he died, and he controlled Leila too. Now
Laila finally came back to life, and she can't be controlled
so she can free the Dajjal"
Uri pushes her out of the chair and slumps down in the
rocking chair.

"Oh well that makes sense, so basically she's a walking
murder machine...right gotcha"
He realises they fell right into the Masih's trap.

"Laila is part of the witches prophecy"

"Yeah, I get it, she will free Him but what I don't fucking
get is why he didn't tell us she'll be after us"
Uri rubs his hands over his face. If she wanted to kill the
Dajjal then she could kill Noah effortlessly he thought.

"That's not all of the prophecy. All the witches are
waiting for Laila because she will betray the Muslims in
the last battle. She will take the side of her true mate"

"The Dajjal" Uri finishes.

"Everybody thinks she will come to save us but she won't"
Amina eyes unsettled by the image in her mind, Laila
standing on her neck and slowly stopping the air from

entering her. Suffocating her to death with one simple move. She lets out a breath she was holding.

"We have to wait for the Masih to tell me what to do next"

"We can't just wait around. If she's woken up and come's after Noah, we need to move"

Uri tries to get up, but Amina quickly puts her knife to his heart.

"It's laced with poison and will paralyze you for ten minutes"

Uri sits back down like a toddler annoyed that he didn't get his way.

"The Queen is still after both of you. Plus, one thing we know for sure is the Masih needs Noah alive. He's been marked to be King since he was a boy so he can't betray us he needs Noah to finish his plan"

She says that with the utmost confidence making Uri slightly relaxed in his seat.

"Fine I'll wait but if a message doesn't come, we'll have to risk being captured by the Queen"

Amina sits on the table.

"Rather her than Laila"

Chapter Eight ~ Life after death.

A beeping sound becoming louder and louder inside my ear drums wakes me up. The smell of flesh and bodily fluids, odours from all kinds were eating at my nostrils.

I open my eyes, my vision adjusting to the colours of the ceiling, a light blue mellow tone. I look around the room I'm in, no one was here but me. A fancy black couch and windows to my right. I was in a hospital room, fancier than the one I was in before. Even the bed was so more comfortable.

I get up to move and my hands and legs feel locked into place. I look at my hands, they were in police cuffs. Even my legs we're locked in them too.

"What the Hell!"

As soon as I say those words a jolt of pain hits my chest and I remember how I got here. How am I alive after what happened? I can feel my heart missing, my body longing for it to come back to its place. I remember being in Amens arms when it happened. I need to call him and ask him why I'm in police cuffs.

"Amen"

No one answers.

"Nala?"

Still, no one answers, I couldn't even hear anyone outside just this damn monitor.

"HELLO"

The monitor starts to beep at a rapid pace, the frustration of not being able to move was making me panic. My heart rate was increasing in the monitor at a high speed, but the noise feels like its chocking out my brain.

I can't stand the noise anymore and I just jump out and punch the monitor, my cuffs breaking from the bed as I do so but there was no more noise. Just peace and the sound of glass hitting the floor.

I sighed and rested my head back on the pillow not knowing what possessed me and how I have the strength to break these but what mattered more was the sound was gone and I could go back to resting.

Nala walks in the room with a bag of chips. Her headphones on her head, she wore a baggy grey jumper that reached above her knees and black leggings. She still looks good without even trying.

She looks at me, my handcuffs broken, and the heart monitor shattered. Her eyes widening by the second.

"Hi" I say.

"Shit shit shit shit"

She closes the door behind her.

"How did you break your cuffs?"

"I don't actually know; I just wanted the noise to stop"

Nala looks at me with dread. The heart monitor completely broken.

"You're gonna be in even worse shit now Leel"

"Is shit like your new word now?"

"That's not funny Laila, your being arrested for being complicit in a murder"

"WHAT your joking right?"

I couldn't resist to laugh.

She looks at the cuffs on my feet.

"Does this look like a joke to you?"

She puts her food down on the couch.

"Why would I be complicit for murder and who's murder?"

Nala bites her lips.

"They think you're helping the serial killer"

"Why would they think that?"

"They knew you, well WE tried to escape, and-"

I sit up on the bed.

"And?"

"The police officer that were with Amen they saw you with the murderer"

"Noah?"

"No, the bald one"

"Uri? What does he have to do with this"?

"Well, they found a video of him at the scene of all the girls deaths. Someone handed in the evidence yesterday and because he was in your room last night, they think you have something to with it"

This couldn't be.

"But he saved you? Did you tell them that he saved you"?

Nala sighs and sits on my bed.

"Yes, I did but they have too much evidence against him"

I touch my chest realising how hollow it is, but I was still alive.

"My heart"

Nala looks at her hands and she plays with her fingers avoiding me.

"Nala, what's wrong?"

"Amen told me what happened before they took him in for questioning"

"Don't tell me he's in trouble?"

"I don't know" she breaths.

She yawns and rubs her eyes to stay awake. Tired wouldn't even come to describing her right now.

"This must be a nightmare Nala"

She just looks at me her shoulders slumped.

"I wish it was"

She reaches to my chest. Touching it. Her hand felt warm, too warm.

"How are you still alive?"

I can feel a tear running down my cheeks. I don't know how I'm alive or how we all deserved to end up here.

"You know how they say Allah test's the ones he loves the most"

I nod my head more tears falling on my cheeks.

"But I don't think He loves us"

She says as she shuts her eyes.

"There's so many voices I just want them to stop, I know I wasn't a good Muslim, but do I really deserve this many voices screaming at me?"

I scoot on the bed and hug her.

"At least you still have a heart" I joke.

Nala laughs. Her cheekbones so high and her small nose creasing at the tip. She was always the cutest girl in school, her smile always so infectious as it shined a bright light around her. Following her wherever she goes.

"How did he take it?"

"He just…ripped it out. It happened so fast. I wish Amen didn't see"

"He called me right after it happened you know. He was screaming. Saying you died"

I can't imagine what he must be going through.

"I want to see him"

"He looks different Leel"

She shakes her head in my shoulder.

"You wouldn't recognise him"

"Why are they questioning him? He hasn't even done anything"

Nala pauses and looks up at me.

"Well, the thing is all the police officers that were with him claimed to not see your heart being taken out by that guy, apparently you just fainted?"

"No, they saw him, they were in the room"

136

"Apparently even the doctors say your fine, but listen I believe Amen, he wouldn't lie about you dying"

"So, what the police think we're making this up?"

Nala nods her head.

"Not me though, Amen begged me to act like I didn't know about your heart once the doctors said your alive"

I reach over to the cuffs on my feet at the end of the bed and rip them out with ease.

Nala just watches me.

"So, are you like one of them now?"

I throw the cuffs on the couch.

"I think so, I don't know how I'm meant to know though. But one thing I know for sure is I want my heart back. It's like I can feel it calling me"

I could hear it beating in my head.

"What does this mean?"

Nala looks me up and down.

"I don't know"

"Your alive but you're not?"

I shrug.

"They were so desperate for me to be like them. Uri kept shouting to Noah to man up and just kill me"

A few nurses pass by the room, and I hold my breath thinking they were going to come in and see the disaster I caused.

Nala however was unfazed like she's completely given up.

"I need paracetamol, my heads killin' me"

She rubs her temples.

"Are the police outside"

Nala smiles at me.

"Yeah, a lot of them, so you can't escape"

"Well, I have to. How are they gonna react to me breaking free from their cuffs"

"Yeah, but I'm completely knackered Laila, I just wanna sleep"

She yawns so loud and plops her head on my lap.

"I feel like I have so much energy though"

My eyes were wide, and my legs were throbbing to move around. My stomach growls in hunger, scratching at the lining to eat.

"Yeah, that's because in the past two days you've been in a comfy hospital bed sound asleep you bitch"

She takes out a snickers bar from her pocket and gives it to me.

"Wait what's your family saying, aren't they worried about you?"

Nala gets up from my lap.

"My brother's managing my dad"

"Are you sure he'll be alright?"

Nala's dad married a second wife after Nala's mum got into a car accident and became paralyzed in bed.

He began to make Nala cook and clean for his second wife like a maid, that's why she got two jobs to stay away from being at home all the time. One in McDonald's and one as a nanny.

Nala and her brother were just waiting to save up so they can move out and live far away from him with their mum. The second wife has a daughter a year younger than Nala who was the epitome of evil.

"He'll be fine"

"And Hoyo"

Nala scrunches her face and hits my head.

"Oh my God don't ever say that you cringe Ayrab"

"I'm not an ayrab I'm a muzlemanity"

Her laughter was filling the room, which is what I wanted. I want to stop time and just have a moment with my best friend.

Someone however had other plans and knocks on the door. Before entering. Two detectives were looking at us in anger. Both were males, one South Asian and one white. They looked at the handcuffs with wide eyes.

"I can explain"

I put my hands up as if I was in a movie.

Nala gives me a dirty look.

'What' I mouth.

"How on earth did you get out of those?" The white detective asks.

"Call for backup"

They both aim their guns at me. If they did shoot me would that even work? I just had my heart removed and I'm here. Nala gets up frightened and lifts her hands up.

"TURN AROUND"

Two Police officers storm in the room and look at the broken chackles in the bed and the broken heart monitor.

"How did you girls do that?"

"GET UP LAILA"

I do as they say and push the covers away from me and get out of the bed. I accidently step on the glass on my bare feet. The glass making its way to my vein. I could smell blood slowly coming out from beneath my feet.

More police officers swarm inside.

"HURRY AND TURN AROUND"

Their guns were pointing at me, and Nala was shaking her eyes closed and her breathing rapid.

The smell of my blood was intoxicating, like how mama would cook, and it would fill the house with a pungent aromatic smell that would eat your nostrils away and make your stomach punch itself in frustration.

"I SAID TURN AROUND YOUNG LADY"

They all had their guns ready to fire at me like I was an Isis member. To be fair a terrorist would be more believable than a murderer.

"Just do as they say" Nala hisses.

I turn around but I'm still stepping on the glass and one sharper glass digs deeper into my flesh. I glance down and a pool of blood is covering my toes. My eyes zoom into the blood that's escaping my feet. A moan nearly escapes my mouth at the feeling. I step on more glass trying to get an even stronger sensation of pain.

It was like scratching an itch you wanted to scratch for a long time.

"HANDS IN THE AIR LAILA, DON'T MAKE ME TELL YOU AGAIN"

I put my hands in the air slowly and I begin to hear a hissing sound, thinking it was Nala but instead it came from my left. It was a black shadow and it had red eyes. It was floating so close to my face.

"Who are you?" I ask.

The police touch both my hand's and begin to put me in handcuffs.

"Don't try to be funny Laila, you're a suspect for first-degree murder"

"I wasn't talking to you" I whisper.

The black shadow moves around me, hissing at me provokingly. I wasn't scared of it, but it was annoyingly teasing me to catch it. I was following it move about to the ceiling and then to the ground, taunting me seeing if id chase it but they've already cuffed me.

The officer pushes me out with Nala, to leave the room and the shadow follows hissing in my ear.

"Stop that" I hiss at the shadow.

"Don't try to resist" the detective warns.

"I said I wasn't talking to you"

The shadow goes into my ear and tickles me. It was irking my skin and provoking me inside my ear.

I move my head to the left to push it out of me, but the police officer holds my head still aggressively.

"Stop moving Miss"

"Somethings in my ear though"

"I Don't care about your ear; stay still as we escort you out of here"

He pushes me out of the room, still barefoot. Smearing the ground with my blood and dragging the glass inside my feet with me.

The shadow begins biting me from the inside. I scream so loud because of the nerve it hit. It was as I'd imagine an electrocution would feel like, Paralyzing me with a large amount of energy shocking the depth of my spine, hitting every bone in my body.

Everyone stops outside the hospital room to look at me scream. Even Nala was gaping at me or not really at me but all their eyes we're on top of me.

"JESUS" someone screams.

Nurses begin to shriek. The police let go of Nala and point their guns on top of my head.

I couldn't really move, my body felt weighed down by something heavy. My back was cracking from the pain of the weight.

I could feel something moving inside my face and mouth. The detective beside me hides behind a police officer.

"EVERYBODY GET BACK"

They all step away from me.

"What is that?" an officer cries.

I wanted to know too. What was on my back. I couldn't turn to look at it or move my arms.

"CALL FOR BACK UP NOW!"

The lights we're dimming in the hallway, and they were all backing away from me very quickly, Nala especially trying to quicken her pace.

I turn to my left; I can see my shadow on the walls. On top of my head was the same shadow I saw with red eyes. It was a bigger shadow in size at least triple the amount. It had smoke raging out of it.

I shake my head this couldn't be happening.

"I want to eat, Laila" it speaks to me.

It's deep voice echoing in my head.

"Feed me"

I look up at it as it stared back at me from above with its eyes that looked like hell. It looks like it's going to eat me if I don't feed it. It's mouth opening and closing in anger, black smoke soaring out of it.

I look in front of me and everyone was running away, yelling uncontrollably. People trying to use the elevator that refused to open. They were stumbling into each other because of the dark like animals, afraid of me or this creature on top of me.

I take a step forward licking my lips feeling dehydrated as hell.

"That's right eat them and then drink from their blood"

I nod my head, it was right. They looked so tasty running away terrified. The creature burning my back making drip in sweat. I can feel my-self about faint, I just wanted to lick them. For once I could just taste their sweet flesh.

My pace quickens as I see the fattest juiciest women. She wore the same clothes I did with a bandage attached to her arm. Her eyes frantic as she limps to get away from me. I feel so happy as I quicken my pace to her. She was so big her fat rolls popping out of her neck.

I can feel the creature also jump around in excitement at the sight of her, his shadow playing around inside my skin frantically.

She was a few steps away from me. I reach out to her and grab her large intestines my hand accidently digging right inside of her stomach. Her screams were so loud it hurt but her smell was so stimulating that I didn't care. I grabbed her intestines taking them out of her body and I licked them. My head was dancing, with the taste as I dangled them on thy neck. I rubbed it all over my face and observe her grabbing her open stomach.in utter horror.

She's crying so much. Bless her sweet soul.

I grab her head twisting it and ending her quickly, so she doesn't suffer anymore. Her body drops and I watch it flop on the floor. The blood was creating a pool, I can swim in for later.

Her head was in my hands, and I look at her for a minute admiring her effort of escaping. Her eyes blinking one last time as I lick her neck. Her veins supplying me with so much life and adrenaline.

A tear slips through my eye. It was so beautiful, so tantalizingly sweet. How could something so perplexingly wonderful become forbidden.

I drop her head feasting on it for far too long that it became dry. Everybody else had escaped the hospital. It was just me and her body, her soul escaping somewhere far. I wonder what she could have done in this life to deserve this end. Poor women. I lay down next to her, my face next to the pool of blood she offers me.

I stick out my tongue and lick and lick till I suck all of it clean. The creature on top of me helping me.

I lay there for a while enjoying the smell of a dead body. It was the same addicting scent of cigarettes, but this was like a real drug, making me feel powerful, all of her energy transforming on to me.

The lights turn back on in the hallway disrupting the tender ambiance.

Footsteps were coming towards me; they were light but quick. I sit up on the floor. Opposite me down the hall was Nala.

I smile at her, I miss her, maybe she could join me.

 "Hi"

I wave at her.

She lifts her hands that were holding a gun. I look at her sideways confused on what she's doing with a gun. There's no way she was going to shoot me, I'm her best friend.

She stalls as she looks at me with so much hate and sadness.

 "Nala put it down, your scaring me"

I go to stand up, but she shoots at me, she misses but she keeps shooting until a bullet lands right at my head. She walks forward and keeps shooting. Some of them miss but one lands right at my eye, blinding me. She shoots one last time before she runs out of bullets and this one went straight to the creature, shutting him off. I could feel him screaming inside my head.

I close my eyes and drop my head on the floor, following after him. My right eye flooding my sockets with blood. The creature melts away inside my face nestling to safety. I can't hear or smell anything. I was just in a state of unwanted sleep as I feel Nala dragging me through the floor.

Chapter Nine ~ The sky is crying

London was experiencing a black out throughout the entire city from Laila's awakening. Her Jinn that were behind her was one of the most powerful to exist thus sucking all of the energy in the city.

Nala pushes her way through the crowd in the dark hospital. She finds a police officer pushing past people in the stairs and she runs after him tackling him to the ground and kicking him in the groin. She snatches his gun and runs the opposite direction. She has to do something so her best friend doesn't hurt herself or anyone else she thought. Nala knew Laila was no longer human, she could feel it when she saw her dead in the hospital when she first arrived. Something inside Nala was telling her Laila wasn't human anymore before she even woke up.

She runs up to the top floor where Laila was and sees her laying on the ground with a dead body. The women's head ripped out of her, and Laila is drenched in a thick dark coated blood. The women's organs were sprawling out next to Laila's leg. Her hijab was matted on to her head and her veins on her face were black.

As if they were tattooed in black paint.

Nala still had her handcuffs on her, but she holds the gun tightly in both hands.

Laila sees her and smiles waving as If nothing happened. She didn't look like Laila the girl she always knew, the one she calls sister. The Laila she confided in and spent every day talking to on the phone when she had a rough day at home. She was just a demon, the voice inside of her warning her. Laila was entirely possessed by that shadow behind her. It's red eyes burnt your own if it looks at you.

"Nala put it down, your scaring me"

Nala ignores the voice inside her telling her not to shoot and aims at Laila's head, till she collapses on the floor.

"Sorry Laila"

She walks over to her still pointing the gun to her face, gagging at the smell and sight in front of her. She's never seen a dead body or the inside of one so naturally she wanted to vomit, but she has no time.

She puts the gun in her pocket and grabs Laila's arms and drags her to the stairs. No one is in the hospital anymore as Laila's body flops down the staircase and Nala sighs at the amount of stairs she has left. It was a long way down, but Nala needed to get her out of here before she hurts someone else. She knew Laila would do the same for her if it was the other way round.

She gets to the ground floor, gasping for air as the lights were still off.

She can finally see clearly from the moonlight shining in through the entrance doors. There was no one in sight but it was loud outside, people were screaming and cheering at the lights going off.

She puts Laila on her back.

"Damn your heavy"

She stumbles as she walks out the entrance doors. An ambulance car door was wide open with the keys still inside. She pushes Laila's body in the passenger's seat, laying her head on the window and shuts the door. She jumps into the driver's seat, her hands finding it hard to start the car with cuffed hands.

146

"Oh my God it can't get worse huh Laila?"
Nala closes her eyes. She refuses to give up now. She drives with her hand on the steering wheel trying her best not to crash into the cars parked in front.
The traffic lights weren't working in the streets, people were driving way above the street limit like caged animals escaping the zoo.

~

Meanwhile in the Middle East especially Jerusalem after Laila's awakening an earthquake began, but not any simple earthquake. The one was shifting large whole's in ground, eating people alive making them sink inside earth's hell. The Queen on the other hand was deep underground on floor -11. The Anesh and Hanesh were in front of her in black suits. The queen was wearing black military boots with a black hooded robe covering her face. Reptilians we're transforming into the shape of humans behind the vampires as they suited up in uniform. All of them rushing with adrenaline drinking freshly caught vampires from the Sahara. It was like they were fed enough blood to last them a year. Curing all of their weaknesses and desires in one go. It was truly a miracle.
"She has awakened" the Queen announces.
Her voice so stern like a Leader should be.
The ceiling rumbles from the earthquake on top of them but they paid no attention. Inner Earth was protected from any earthquakes happening on the surface to the humans.
There were thousands of creatures in front of the Queen. Witches and wizards, faces all covered even to their eyes.
"We must not let her conquer Jerusalem if she does so our Kingdom will be destroyed. Noah and Aaliyah must mate otherwise the fate of our Lord will be no more"
Her jinn on her back peering at the army in front of her with joy.

147

"I shall not let my kingdom be ruined. In the power of our Lord and saviour Iblis, we shall protect our kind. NOW GO AND FIND NOAH AND HIS MATE, BRING THEM TO ME BUT NOT IN PEICES"

There were a hundred elevators around the room each using it to go up to the first floor. Once the Queen was left alone, she turns to her serpent slivering through the ceiling. There was a tree the serpent liked to nestle in, by the corner of the Queens throne. It had five branches with no leaves.
  "Well done" the serpent hisses batting her long eyelashes.
  "The dajjal will reward you for your servicesss"
The Queen clenches her jaw and opens a portal to a different dimension, she walks through it her face changing to lizard as she does so, and it quickly closes after her.

~

In the cabin where Noah and Uri seek refuge, the walls begin to shake so much breaking down the ceiling wood frames.
  "We have to get out of here"
A gust of wind breaks through the window the shadow people wailing in pain. Their bodies flying all through the cabin attacking at it with full force.
  "We have to wait for the Masih"
"Fuck the Masih we're going to be eaten alive if we stay here" Uri shouts.
He grabs Noah and puts him on his back.
  "Take us back to the station"
Amina runs to the door and puts her body on it.
  "BUT THE QUEEN" she protests.
The shadow people break through the furniture and Uri sighs pushing her out of the way.
  "Fuck her too"

148

He kicks down the door and Amina follows after him, attacking the shadow people with her knife.

The trees where crying and wailing.

"Shadow people weren't always this violent?"

"They can be when a strong demon is awakened"

She didn't have to say Laila's name.

They get to the station doors, but it's locked, the lights and engine stopped working because of Laila.

"Why isn't it open?"

"It must be her demon it's shutting down our energy down here"

"Come on you must know a spell or two to get it working, at least the doors get them to open up before those things come after us"

He looks back at the forest, the shadow people were chaotic, the trees were shattering the cabin till it was a flat surface.

Amina closes her eyes and puts her hands on the doors of the station. She focuses all of her power sucking out the last bit of energy she has pushing it out into the station doors. The opaque doors slowly open just enough for Uri to run inside but her energy completely sucks the life out of her, and she collapse on the soil shutting the doors. Uri puts down Noah and runs after Amina, but he couldn't reach her in time. Her body was limp as she lays on the ground of the forest. Her eyes shut not seeing the shadow people run towards her body slamming themselves on top of her.

Uri watches from the inside of the station as they feast on her one by one and slowly her body was merging into one of them.

"No, No, No!"

He slams his fist on the door.

"GET OF HER"

Her body slowly fades away until she became one of them, a shadow.

"No Amina"

149

Uri begins tears up as he stops slamming on the door and watches her shadow walk away into the forest.
He puts his face on the door and breaths heavily, tears slowly consuming his face.

Chapter 10 – Amen don't.

Nala parks a few doors down from her house, parking in the middle of the street, it was the best she could do being cuffed. Laila was still passed out in the passenger seat her head flopping from side to side as Nala was driving at a hazardous speed.

She Gets out the car, There were people out of their homes to see what was happening. Neighbours complaining about the Blackout.

She opens the passenger's seat and Laila drops on her back. Her neighbour sees her, an old nosy white lady who had a chair outside her house. She was too old to even see properly.

"What ya got there?"

"Just my bag ha-ha"

Nala smiles and walks ahead.

She gets to her door, she could her stepsister and brother all shouting in the house. It was a four bedroom, but it still felt too tight for Nala to live inside.

She walks over to the Garden; it wasn't attached to the neighbours. There was a pathway to get to the door of the garden. She pushes Laila over the door with all her might but fails.

"Nala?"

She turns around startled to see her brother.

"Oh my God Moh, you scared me; hurry open the door"

He looks at Laila who's smothered in dried blood wearing a hospital gown.

"ALLAH"

"Moh please I need to get to the shed without baba finding out"

"Why does she look like that?"

He opens the door with his keys.

"I'll explain later"

"Wasn't she arrested? it's all over the news"

Moh helps Nala carry her into the shed and he notices her handcuffs.

"Where you arrested too?"

The garden lights coming on briefly as they go into the shed and place her on the floor. He wipes his hands on Nala's jumper.

It was a messy shed just filled with gardening tools and old furniture and a few old things their mum used to own till there dad chucked it out here.

"Yeah, like I said I'll explain later. I need to call Amen right now"

Moh gets out his lighter.

"Seriously?"

"I'm too stressed from the blackout, ain't no way I'm not bunning' tonight"

The smell of weed was wafting through Laila's nostrils awakening her senses ever so slowly.

"Alright stay here I'm gonna call Amen"

She gets out the gun in her pocket and hands it to her brother.

"Oh, and if she wakes up and tries to kill you just shoot her, trust me she won't die"

He stares at her, speechless as she gets out her phone and goes behind the shed.

She rings Amens phone and he picks up right away.

"Amen" she breaths.
"Amen I need you right now, where are you?"
He doesn't respond. There was a buzzing sound through the phone.
"Hey, can you hear me"
"Hi"
"Are you good? where are you?"
He coughs through the phone.
"Yeah, I'm fine, they let me go right before the blackout"
He was so monotone, and Nala notices.
He coughs again.
"Where's Laila?" he asks gently.
He was never this quiet when he spoke with her. A voice inside Nala whispers telling her to be weary of Amen.
"What do you mean where's Laila, you left her in the hospital remember?"
Amen goes silent for a second.
"Is she still in the hospital?"
"Amen"
"Yes"
"What's wrong? why you acting so...so weird?"
"Just tell me where she is Nala" His voice sounded strained.
Nala's breaths are shaky as she hears Amens voice. It didn't sound like him.
"Amen are you okay? Is this really you? Please because I really need you right now before she wakes up, I need you to help me please" she cries.
"Nala tell me where she is"
A gunshot goes off startling Nala and making her ears ring.
"NALA WHAT WAS THAT"
She hangs up the phone and runs to the shed.

~

153

Amen was sitting down in a dark room, he was in his police uniform. He was completely knackered not sleeping for two nights straight. There is a black desk in front of him his phone on the table on loudspeaker as Nala speaks. He notices her voice so shaky. He loves her so much that he couldn't believe what he was doing to her. Opposite him sat four detectives, listening into his conversation.
His phone was on the table. His eye bags deep in insomnia. He looks completely distraught as he sighs loudly when they hang up the phone.
"You got it?"
"Yeah, 13 park avenue"
"Right let's go"
The detectives get up to leave the room.
  "You did good Amen, we'll get your sister the help she needs"
Amen doesn't respond or look at them.
They shut the door leaving him alone as he bangs his head on the table till its bruised. He shuts his eyes imagining Nala's face when she realises what he's done. She will never forgive him, and he knows it.

~

Meanwhile in the Dajjals cave, it was empty, the chains that were once on his body were scattered everywhere around the cave. As everyone in the world dealt with the awakening of such dark matter, the island was peaceful not a thing inside it. Only Laila's blood sample was in the centre of where the Masih resided and was completely ridden empty of its matter.

The End of book 1.

The second book is under investigation by the Queen.

Acknowledgments

Thank you to the most creative artist Yusuf Saib (@e.f.y. u)
For the most breath-taking book cover I could possibly ask
for. He has utterly captured the true essence of Laila in her
final form, a demon by blood. No words can describe how
grateful I am to have worked with such a detailed
imaginative artist.
Thank you, Yusuf, for bringing Laila to life.

Printed in Great Britain
by Amazon